A secret.

"You could make Wayne Miller a valentine that says 'Get lost,' and sign it, 'Your Secret Un-Admirer,' " Stephanie sputtered.

"Don't even say *valentine* and his name in the same sentence!" Lauren shrieked.

Listening to Lauren's reaction to Wayne liking her made me even more uneasy about giving Henry a valentine. Just thinking about it made my stomach start to hurt. What if he didn't like me the same way I liked him? It would definitely have to be a secret.

Look for these and other books
in the Sleepover Friends Series:

A Valentine for Patti

Susan Saunders

AN
APPLE
PAPERBACK

SCHOLASTIC INC.
New York Toronto London Auckland Sydney

ISBN 0-590-43927-8

Copyright © 1991 by Daniel Weiss Associates, Inc. All rights reserved. Published by Scholastic Inc. APPLE PAPERBACKS is a registered trademark of Scholastic Inc. SLEEPOVER FRIENDS is a registered trademark of Daniel Weiss Associates Inc.

12 11 10 9 8 7 6 5 4 3 2 1   0 1 2 3 4 5/9

Printed in the U.S.A.   28

First Scholastic printing, January 1991

Chapter 1

Well, I guess it's my turn now.

I'm kind of nervous about this. But since Stephanie, Lauren, and Kate have already told you about us, I suppose it's only fair that I do, too. I guess I should start by telling you about myself. I'm Patti Jenkins. I was named after my great-great-grandmother Patricia, but I'd rather go by Patti. No one's called Patricia anymore!

I live with my parents and my little brother Horace. I know, I know — where did my parents come up with these names? It's a good thing there aren't any more kids in the family, or one of them would be named Gertrude! I have a cat named Adelaide, and I like all kinds of animals. I'm tall — way too tall, if you ask me — and skinny and I have light brown hair. That's it for me!

Oh, except that I'm in Mrs. Mead's class, 5B, at Riverhurst Elementary with my best friends: Lauren Hunter, Stephanie Green, and Kate Beekman — otherwise known as the Sleepover Friends!

That's where we were one Monday morning when Mrs. Mead said she had a very important announcement to make. I looked at Henry Larkin, who sits across the aisle from me. He shrugged. "Maybe they're going to give us our winter vacation early?" he whispered.

Kate and Lauren sit next to each other in the second row, and Stephanie sits in front of Kate. I'm stuck way back in the last row — the only good thing about it is that I *do* get to sit next to Henry.

Mrs. Mead went on. "Three weeks from now is one of my favorite holidays," she said. "Valentine's Day!"

"*That*'s the big announcement?" Henry Larkin joked.

I giggled. Henry always has a funny comment to make. That's one of the reasons I like him. Henry also has brown hair, big blue eyes, and he's pretty decent, for a fifth-grader. Most of the other guys in our class are hopeless.

"No." Mrs. Mead smiled at Henry. "I was getting to that. The fifth- and sixth-grade teachers thought you all needed a break from the coldest winter in thirty-five years, and since Valentine's Day is coming up we decided to have a party here at school!"

"All right!" Stephanie cried. She loves parties. They give her another excuse to buy clothes.

Lauren turned and grinned at me. But Kate was raising her hand.

"What kind of party?" she asked Mrs. Mead. That's Kate for you — she always wants to know all the details. She was probably making a file on the party already!

"Well," Mrs. Mead replied, "since the last time we had a winter this cold was in 1956, we thought it would be fun to have a fifties sock hop!"

"We have to hop around in our socks?" Karla Stamos asked.

Stephanie turned around and rolled her eyes at me. "Talk about dense," she mouthed.

"It's what they called dance parties back then," Mrs. Mead explained. "Back when I was a teenager, we had them all the time."

"Why are they called sock hops?" asked Mark Freedman. He's another boy in our class who's okay to talk to.

"Because people used to take off their shoes to

dance in their socks," Stephanie said. She's a really good dancer and she knows a lot about music and stuff like that.

"That sounds great!" Jane Sykes said.

"Now, the fifth grade will be in charge of decorating the gym and providing refreshments," Mrs. Mead continued. "The sixth grade will handle all of the music, and they'll also find judges for the best-costume contest."

"What do you mean — costumes?" Henry asked with a grimace. "This is Valentine's Day, not Halloween!"

"This is a fifties party, Henry," Mrs. Mead said patiently, "so I expect to see all of you dressed as if it were 1956! And if I recall correctly, you've already done this once before."

A couple of people snickered. Mrs. Mead was referring to the Homecoming parade, when Henry was on the float that Kate, Lauren, Stephanie, and I put together, along with Ginger Kinkaid and Christy Soames. The float was called "Riverhurst School Through the Years," and we had all dressed as students from different decades. Henry and I had dressed as kids from the fifties. Henry had greased his hair back and worn a leather jacket and jeans.

Mrs. Mead clapped her hands together. "Okay, we have some more business to take care of before class gets started for the day. We need to elect a decorations chairperson to represent 5B. He or she will work with the chairpersons from 5A and 5C and be in charge of decorating the gym. Would anyone like to make a nomination?"

Lauren raised her hand immediately. "I nominate Stephanie Green."

I smiled at Stephanie. She's terrific at drawing, painting, and designing. Everyone knew that — her artwork was always being hung up in some hallway.

Mrs. Mead nodded. "Any other nominations?"

"How about Mark Freedman?" Henry said in a serious voice. Then he burst out laughing.

I giggled. Mark is as good an artist as I am — terrible!

Even Mrs. Mead was trying not to laugh. "Okay, then," she said, "we have Stephanie and Mark on the ballot. Anyone else?" When no one answered, she said, "Everyone who thinks Stephanie should be 5B's decorations chairperson, raise your hand."

I raised mine, and so did almost everyone else in the class — including Mark.

"Who's for Mark?" Mrs. Mead asked.

Jenny Carlin raised her hand but when she saw she was the only one, her face turned bright red. She was just voting for Mark because she didn't like Stephanie!

"Then it's settled. Congratulations, Stephanie! I'll need to meet with you after school tomorrow to start planning, okay?"

Stephanie nodded.

"Who's going to be in charge of refreshments?" Jenny asked.

"How about Lauren!" Kate suggested with a grin. She always teases Lauren about eating so much. It's not as if Lauren's overweight — just the opposite. But it seems like she's always hungry. Kate calls her the Bottomless Pit. Kate's short, though — she doesn't understand how hungry you get when you're growing. Both Lauren and I are pretty tall, and I, for one, keep getting taller.

Lauren punched Kate on the arm. "No fair!" she said.

Mrs. Mead tapped a pen against her desk. "We'll also need to organize the refreshments and get some parents to chaperon. I'll hand out some forms for you to take home and fill out. Now, let's get on with — "

Mrs. Mead didn't get on with anything, because at that moment the door opened and a girl came into our classroom.

"Oh, hello, Hope!" Mrs. Mead said warmly. "I forgot you were starting today."

The girl just stood there without saying anything. She was dressed in a really funky outfit — she had on a tie-dyed shirt, an Indian-print skirt, and leather moccasins.

But the most noticeable thing about her was her hair. It was the longest hair I had ever seen — inches past her waist. It was blonde, and it was braided into about a hundred different little braids. I'd never seen anything like it.

"Class, I'd like you to welcome Hope Lenski," Mrs. Mead said. "Hope, this is 5B — I'm sure you'll get to know everyone by the end of the week. Now, let's see . . . Hope, why don't you sit over here, next to Karla."

Hope took her seat and started rummaging in her flowered knapsack.

"Well, then, let's get started on the math homework!" Mrs. Mead said cheerfully.

"Have you ever heard of someone transferring in *January*?" Stephanie remarked when the four of us sat down at our usual table in the cafeteria.

Kate shook her head. "Never."

"There must be some special reason," Lauren commented. She took a big bite of her turkey sandwich.

"Like what?" Stephanie wondered.

"Maybe her parents were transferred by their jobs," I said. "Lots of times companies send people to different towns." My family had moved three or four times because of that. My parents are university professors who have gone from school to school. Not too long ago, we almost moved to Alaska!

"Don't you think they would have done it at Christmastime when we were all on vacation?" asked Kate. "That would be the sensible thing to do."

"Well, Horace's teachers moved him up a grade in school, and that was only a couple of weeks ago," I pointed out. My brother is such a genius that he was put into the second grade because first grade was too slow for him.

"Yes, but he started in second grade when everyone went back to school after the holidays," Kate argued. "*That* makes sense."

"I think it's great to have someone new in our class," Lauren said. "I get tired of looking at the same bunch of heads in front of me."

"Thanks a lot!" Stephanie said.

"I didn't mean you," Lauren laughed. "Anyway, the last time someone new came into our class it turned out pretty good." She smiled at me. I had moved to Riverhurst at the beginning of fifth grade.

"Pretty well, you mean," Kate corrected her.

Lauren rolled her eyes and took another bite of her sandwich.

Kate and Lauren grew up in Riverhust and

they've been best friends practically forever, even though they're complete opposites.

They began having sleepovers when they were in the first grade. Fortunately, it's a tradition that's lasted! So when Stephanie moved to town in fourth grade, she became part of the Sleepover Friends — and then I did this year.

Stephanie and I both used to live in the city. We knew each other when we were six, if you can believe that! But she and I are no more alike than Kate and Lauren are. I didn't recognize Stephanie when I first saw her again — she'd changed a lot in four years. I guess I have, too, but mostly I'm just taller. The big thing in Stephanie's life now is that she has a new baby brother and sister — twins! She didn't like it at first, but she's gotten used to being a big sister.

"So, Miss Decorations Chairperson, what are you planning for the dance?" Lauren asked Stephanie.

Stephanie took a sip of apple juice, then tapped her chin with her finger. "I'm not sure yet."

"I know!" said Lauren. "I see something in a red . . . with a little black, and maybe some white!" Red, black, and white is Stephanie's favorite combination. Almost everything she wears is in those colors.

Stephanie laughed. "Well, it *is* a Valentine's dance. I mean, we *have* to have red! I can't believe we're having a dance with sixth-graders," she said dreamily. She gazed around the cafeteria. "What if we actually get to dance with them?"

Lauren smiled. "Picture this . . . Stephanie standing by the record player . . . suddenly, a slow song comes on, and Taylor Sprouse glides up to her, slicks back his hair, and says, 'Hey beautiful, let's dance!' "

We all burst out laughing.

"Now *that* I have to see!" said Kate between giggles.

Taylor Sprouse is a boy in the sixth grade whom Kate used to like — and now Stephanie has a major crush on him. He's good-looking but incredibly conceited. Kate's in the Video Club with him.

Stephanie folded her arms across her chest. "It could happen," she said defensively.

"In your dreams!" Lauren teased her.

Just then I spotted Hope Lenski standing in the middle of the lunch room holding a tray. "Look, there's the new girl," I said.

Before I could stand up to ask Hope to come sit with us, she turned and walked over to the opposite end of the cafeteria.

"She doesn't seem very friendly," Stephanie said.

"Maybe she's shy," Lauren suggested.

"It's not easy to meet people," I told them. "Especially when you're transferring in the middle of the year."

"What's her name again?" asked Stephanie.

"Hope Lenski," I said.

"That's kind of a funny name — Hope," said Kate. "She must get teased about it a lot."

"What about those clothes?" Stephanie shook her head. "She looks just like I did on the Homecoming float! The only thing missing is the headband."

Stephanie had dressed as someone from the early seventies, with a headband, a tie-dyed T-shirt, and bell-bottom jeans with patches all over them.

"Well, we'll find out more about her soon enough. Just like Mrs. Mead said — by the end of the week we'll all be friends," I reminded them.

"I still think her showing up *now* is weird," said Kate.

"Maybe she wanted to transfer for the incredibly fantastic Valentine's party, which is going to be a huge success, thanks to *moi*!" said Stephanie.

"Yeah, right," Kate mumbled.

"You're just cranky because you're not in charge, for once!" Stephanie said with a knowing grin.

11

It's true that Kate is usually the one who tells the rest of us what to do. She directed the Homecoming float and a home movie starring the Sleepover Friends — which actually won a prize!

Kate wrinkled her nose at Stephanie's suggestion, and I wondered how she was going to like standing on the sidelines. If I knew Kate, not very much!

Chapter
2

"Did you think of anything for the gym decorations yet?" Kate asked Stephanie. It was Tuesday and we were talking before class started.

"Kate, I only found out yesterday that I was doing it," Stephanie replied.

Kate shrugged. "I know, but I was wondering if you'd done any work on it last night."

Stephanie shook her head. "I had too much homework."

"Still, there's not much time to organize. Do you need some help?"

Stephanie put her hands on her hips and her eyes got very round. I could tell she thought Kate was butting in.

"I'm sure you'll think of something terrific," I

told Stephanie quickly. "Did you find out who the other two chairpersons are yet?"

She nodded. "Tracy Osner and Bobby Krieger — which is great, because they're both really easy to work with."

Kate sat down at her desk and started arranging her pens and pencils. She wasn't enjoying not being the center of attention. Plus, a long time ago, she had had a crush on Bobby Krieger.

"You're going to get other people to help you, though, right?" Kate asked.

"I guess so." Stephanie gestured with her head toward the door. "Look who's here — the mystery girl."

Hope walked into the room.

"Let's go say hi to her," Lauren suggested.

Kate jumped out of her chair. "Good idea!"

We walked over to Hope's desk. I hoped she wouldn't feel like we were ganging up on her.

As usual, Kate led the way. "Hi," she said brightly. "I'm Kate Beekman. We want to welcome you to Riverhurst!"

"And to 5B," said Lauren, "which, incidentally, is the best class in the whole school. I'm Lauren Hunter."

Hope looked overwhelmed. "Hi," was all she

said. Today she was wearing jeans and a big flannel shirt that looked like it belonged to an older brother, and she had a scarf tied around her hair. With that big scarf on and her clothes so baggy, you could hardly even see her.

"This is Stephanie Green," Kate continued, "and Patti Jenkins."

I smiled at her. "Hi." I'm a little shy about meeting people, too.

"I'm working on the decorations for the fifties sock hop," said Stephanie. "Maybe you can help with them. It'll be a lot of fun, and you'll get to meet lots of kids from the other classes."

"Oh, okay, I guess," Hope said.

"Well, you probably want to get ready for class," Kate said to Hope. "We'll see you later." That was our cue to leave.

"She doesn't seem very friendly," Stephanie said softly as we walked away.

"I think she's just shy," I said.

"I think she's *weird*," Kate whispered from in back of us.

That's Kate for you — she makes up her mind about people in about two seconds. I hoped she would give the new girl a chance — the same chance she had given me!

15

* * *

I don't know about you, but my favorite subject is science. I really enjoy studying the natural world and the environment. I'm in a club at school called the Quarks, and we meet once a week. We work on projects — experiments and inventions, mostly — and take trips to the science museum, where they always have at least one cool exhibit. Sometimes kids at school tease me about being a "Quarkhead," but I don't really care. I wouldn't give up the Quarks for anything.

That week our class was discussing the weather, partly because that was the section we'd gotten to in our textbook, and partly because it had been affecting our lives so much! It had been so cold that Adelaide, my cat, wouldn't even go outside. She usually loves to romp around in the yard — but not lately! She's been curled up in a ball on the couch every day and hasn't moved unless it's time to eat. That's the way we were *all* feeling about the cold weather.

Mrs. Mead was showing us how to read a barometer. That's something that measures the pressure in the atmosphere and tells you if the air is damp or dry and stuff like that.

"Does anyone know what it means if the needle on the barometer is falling?" Mrs. Mead asked.

"It's time to get a new battery for it!" Henry joked. I couldn't help smiling.

Mrs. Mead shook her head. "No. Thank you, Henry," she said. "Anyone else?"

I thought I knew, but I wasn't sure. I didn't want to say the wrong answer, so I kept quiet.

Just then I saw Hope raise her hand.

"Yes, Hope?" Mrs. Mead turned toward her.

"Um, it means that bad weather is on the way — probably rain or some other form of precipitation," Hope said quietly.

That's what I thought! I almost said.

"You're right," Mrs. Mead said. "A low pressure system means bad weather, and high pressure indicates a clear sky, and good weather."

"If a barometer tells you that much, then why do we need weather forecasters on TV?" Lauren wondered out loud.

Mrs. Mead laughed. "Now, another indicator of the weather is clouds. Can anyone tell me what types of clouds there are?"

Again, Hope raised her hand — before I had a chance to answer. "Cirrus, cumulus, nimbus, and stratus," she said quickly.

Mrs. Mead nodded. "Very good, Hope."

"So she's weird and she's a brain," Henry whispered.

I frowned at him. I was impressed. Hope really knew a lot about science! I wondered if maybe she would want to join the Quarks Club. She hadn't seemed too enthusiastic about helping with the decorations, so I wasn't sure. Maybe she didn't like joining school clubs for some reason. But I decided I would ask her, if I had a chance.

After lunch that day we trooped down to the art studio for art class.

"Hello," Ms. Gilberto said cheerfully. "Take an easel and get started! Today we are learning how to draw animals," Ms. Gilberto announced. She gestured to a table in the middle of the studio that was piled high with magazines. "Pick out a picture you like and try to copy it, or else interpret an animal in your own way."

We all went over to the table and searched for pictures in the magazines, except for Stephanie, who started drawing right away. I decided to try to draw a bear. We each chose easels and started drawing. Lauren and I like to stand next to each other because we're both pretty bad at art. She's famous for turning clay into completely useless shapes, and I hold the record for the most confusing painting ever.

About ten minutes later, Hope wandered into

the room — and I mean wandered. She really looked lost!

"I'm sorry," she said to Ms. Gilberto. "I'm new here and I couldn't find the studio."

Ms. Gilberto guided her over to the desk and checked her in on the attendance sheet. "What a lovely name, Hope," she said, smiling. "Now, Hope, there is an empty easel right here." She pointed to the one next to Stephanie. "You may draw whatever animal you like — from a picture or from memory. It's up to you!"

Hope nodded and walked over to the easel.

I sure wouldn't want to stand next to Stephanie in art class. Her work is so good that it makes mine look ten times worse than it already is! She even painted part of the mural on the studio wall.

I spent the rest of class concentrating on shading my bear so that the fur looked natural. Drawing all of the little bristles took forever.

"All right, people!" Ms. Gilberto called out. "Only a few minutes left. Please put your names on your drawings and leave them on my desk. We'll discuss them next time." She beamed at all of us. "Perhaps we can post them in the hallways and have our very own animal kingdom."

"Yeah, right," Lauren murmured, staring at her

picture of her kitten Rocky — at least I think it was Rocky. "Maybe there's some room in the second grade for this!"

Stephanie tore off her drawing of a tiger. Then she turned to look at Hope's picture. Hope was putting the finishing touches on a family of mice. Her sketch reminded me of something in a science textbook — it was incredibly realistic.

"That's really nice," Stephanie said to Hope.

"Yeah, you're good," I added.

"Thanks," Hope mumbled.

"You must have had good art teachers at your last school," Stephanie said.

Hope shrugged. "Not really," she said. She kept drawing. I guess she wanted to make it perfect, since it was her first project for Ms. Gilberto.

"I can't believe her!" Stephanie complained once we left the studio to go back to 5B — without Hope. "Doesn't she want to be friends with anybody?"

"It doesn't seem like it," Lauren remarked. "Every time we talk to her she barely answers us."

"She's still adjusting to a new school," I said in Hope's defense.

"She could be one of those loner types," Kate said. "Like the girl in this movie I saw last night — she kept to herself, only she had this journal she wrote in all the time, and then some kids at school found the journal and — "

"Enough already!" Lauren said. "We're talking about Hope, not some actress in a movie."

Stephanie snapped her fingers. "That's it! She's famous, and that's why she's being so quiet and secretive about everything. And she's dressing like that so no one will recognize her!"

"Give me a break!" Kate said, rolling her eyes. "You guys have been reading too many issues of *Star Turns*."

"And you've been watching too many movies!" Stephanie said.

"Well, I still think she's weird," said Kate.

"That's okay — she probably thinks you are, too," said Stephanie, grinning.

I know what you're thinking — my friends are *all* weird! And when they get excited about something, I can hardly get a word in edgewise. But trust me, they're great friends.

Chapter
3

"On your marks . . . get set . . . dig in!" Lauren shouted. She was standing in the doorway holding a bowl of freshly popped cheese popcorn.

"Put it down already," said Kate.

We were sitting on the floor in my bedroom, ready for our Friday night pig-out, a sleepover tradition. I like school, but I'm always glad when the weekend rolls around. It's definitely something to celebrate!

Lauren sat down and we all grabbed handfuls of popcorn. "I brought some of my mom's cookies, too," said Stephanie.

"Good — this is going to be a long night," said Lauren.

"What do you mean?" I asked her. "Longer than

usual for a Friday night?" We stay up late at every sleepover.

"We have a lot more to talk about this week," Lauren said, taking a sip of Dr Pepper. "First of all, *what* are we going to wear to that sock hop thing?"

"Don't ask me!" I said.

"We could always get the same clothes we wore for the float," said Kate.

"No, that would be boring," said Stephanie. She grinned. "I already have my outfit picked out."

"No fair!" Lauren exclaimed. "You always know what to wear! Hand over those cookies. We have some serious thinking to do."

I grabbed one of the peanut-butter-chocolate-chip cookies from Stephanie's paper plate and took a big bite. It was delicious, as usual. "Maybe you can borrow something from your mother," I told Lauren.

"She's not old enough," Lauren complained. "Nope, it looks like I'll have to rent from Clothing Classics again."

"Not necessarily," said Stephanie, twirling a lock of her long curly hair around her finger. "You can probably improvise with the clothes you have."

"*I* can't, but you probably could. So when are you coming over to my house?" Lauren asked with a grin.

"How about next week, at the sleepover?" Stephanie suggested. "The dance will be a week away and we can have a dress rehearsal."

"Great — I'll bring my camera," said Kate. "*Vogue* might want some photos of the latest fashions in Riverhurst."

I started laughing. "That'll be the day!"

"Okay — next topic of discussion," said Lauren, pretending to check off an imaginary list the way Kate always does. "Boys."

"What about them?" Stephanie asked. "Do you have a crush on someone new?"

"Or are you finally going to stop playing hard to get and go out with Wayne Miller?" Kate joked.

We all cracked up laughing, except Lauren. "That is seriously not funny," she said. "Don't even wish that on me!"

Wayne Miller is in our class, and he's about the most disgusting fifth-grade boy in Riverhurst — and probably in the whole state! He's always doing gross things, like burping extra loudly in the cafeteria, or catching flies and pulling off their wings. So when Lauren found out he has a crush on her she practically died!

"What if he asks you to *dance*?" Stephanie howled.

"With my luck he will!" Lauren wailed. "Why

24

do these things happen to me?" She lay down and put her face into her pillow.

"Lauren Miller . . ." Kate mused. "It has a nice ring to it."

Lauren picked up the pillow and bashed Kate over the head with it. "Cut it out or I'll tell Taylor Sprouse you're madly in love with him!" she threatened.

"Speaking of Taylor . . . do you guys think any of the boys will actually dance with the girls at this Valentine's party?" Stephanie asked.

"I think that if the music's good, then everybody will dance," Lauren said.

"I agree." I nodded. "I wish you were in charge of the music, too," I told Stephanie. "Who knows what the sixth grade will come up with?"

"It's going to be old songs from the fifties," Lauren said. "Does anyone know what that music was even like?"

"I have an idea!" I said. "My mom has a tape of the top songs from the fifties. We can borrow it and play it at Lauren's next week to practice dancing."

"Great idea!" Stephanie said.

"We'll be ready for that party whether those stupid boys are or not!" Kate said.

"Sometimes they act like they're in second grade

instead of sixth," Lauren commented.

"That reminds me," I said. "There's something I wanted to talk to you guys about. You know how I told you that Horace skipped into the second grade, right?"

"Sure," said Lauren. "How's he doing?"

"Not so good," I admitted. Horace had been in a bad mood all week and that night after dinner I had finally found out why. I overheard him talking to my mom and dad, telling them that a group of boys at school had been making fun of him. I got the impression they were pushing him around a little, too, though he didn't say that. I knew he wasn't telling my parents the whole story. I explained it all to Lauren, Kate, and Stephanie.

"Wow," said Lauren. "So he's being bullied by his classmates. That's terrible!"

"I know!" I said. "I even heard Horace say that he doesn't want to go back there on Monday — in fact, he wants to quit school altogether!"

"You're kidding! But he's so smart! On the other hand, he *is* pretty small compared to the other second-graders," Kate commented.

"Well, I don't think they're *hurting* him. At least they better *not* be!" I said angrily. I saw surprised looks on my friends' faces. I usually don't get so heated up about things. But this was my little brother! I hated to see him so miserable.

"Do you think they should move him back to first grade?" Kate asked.

I shook my head. "No, he's too smart for first grade. He doesn't belong there," I said gloomily.

Stephanie laid her hand on my arm. "I know you're worried about him, Patti, but Horace can take care of himself. He's so smart he'll think of a way to put those jerks in their place!"

I nodded. "You're probably right." I hoped so, anyway.

"Okay!" Kate picked up the remote and flicked on the TV. "Next item on the agenda — 'Friday Night Chillers'!"

It was ten o'clock when the movie ended. We turned on the radio and decided to play a game of Mad Libs. But first, Lauren and I went downstairs to get some more munchies.

We were walking back upstairs with four bowls of ice cream when I heard a strange sound coming from Horace's bedroom. I stopped in the hallway and listened.

Lauren stopped beside me.

Sure enough, Horace was crying — which

made me feel like crying, too. Then I heard my mother saying, "It's going to be all right, honey, it's going to be all right." I peeked in the door and saw my mother rubbing Horace's back, as he cried into his pillow.

I turned around and faced Lauren. "It's those stupid second-graders' fault," I muttered angrily. Seeing how upset Horace was made me even more worried. What was going to happen to him if he couldn't stand up to them?

"He'll be okay," she assured me. "You'll see."

"I hope so," I said.

Chapter
4

"Good morning. Did everyone remember to bring in their sign-up sheets for the sock hop?" Mrs. Mead asked on Monday.

We all started digging in our bookbags and totes. I saw Henry pulling a crumpled, torn, piece of paper out of his back pocket. Boys are so hopeless. Even when they're cute.

I felt someone's eyes on me, and looked up to see Kate staring at me. Then she motioned her head slightly in Hope's direction. I followed her gaze and saw Hope sitting scrunched down in her seat, looking down at the ground. What was going on with her?

Even Mrs. Mead noticed. "Hope," she said gently. "Do you have your note?"

Hope didn't look up. She just sighed, reached into her knapsack, and pulled out a carefully folded piece of paper. I looked back at Kate, and she shrugged.

Mrs. Mead took Hope's note and read it. "Oh, how nice," she said. "You're going to contribute some chips and guacamole dip. And your dad has offered to chaperon. Please thank him for me, Hope." Hope just nodded miserably.

After Mrs. Mead had collected our forms, she started talking about our math homework from the night before so I got out my notebook and looked at the problems.

I couldn't concentrate, though. I kept picturing Horace in *his* class and wondering how his morning was going. We had spent Sunday together, sledding at the park. Whenever I asked him about school, he said he didn't want to talk about it. I knew things were serious then — Horace doesn't usually hide things from me.

Anyway, we'd had a great time, and he seemed to be in a much happier mood. Until that morning when it was time to leave for school. He had eaten breakfast at a snail's pace, and my mother practically had to drag him out to the car.

I looked down at my notebook. While I'd been thinking about Horace, I had doodled his name all over my homework. Mrs. Mead was going to think I was crazy!

* * *

"What are you going to bring?" Lauren asked me on our way to the lunchroom that day. "Some of that great onion-and-chives dip?"

I shook my head. "No, I'm going to make brownies."

As soon as we sat down at our usual table, Kate turned to us and said, "Well? What do you think?"

Lauren, Stephanie, and I looked at each other. "What are you talking about?" asked Stephanie.

Kate looked amazed. "About *Hope*, silly! What is her problem?"

"Oh, you mean with the note and her dad and all?" Lauren asked.

Kate nodded. "If you ask me, it's kind of weird for her *dad* to be the one to chaperon. I mean, moms usually do that kind of stuff."

I couldn't see what the big deal was. "Maybe her mom has to work that night or something," I said. Lauren and Stephanie nodded, but Kate didn't look satisfied.

"I still think it's weird," she muttered.

We ended up right behind Jenny Carlin and her best friend Angela Kemp on the lunchline. Jenny is one of the only people in my class I have to admit I just don't like. She's always putting me and my friends down, or competing with us, or something! And Angela goes along with whatever Jenny does. They were talking about Hope, too. Jenny was saying, "I wonder if the new girl's dad is as weird as she is."

Angela snickered. "I bet he is," she said. "He probably has long hair and a beard down to his waist."

"She's too much," Jenny said disdainfully.

"I just hope her chips and dip are edible," Angela said.

It bothered me that everyone kept using the word "weird" to describe Hope. No one even knew her yet! All we knew was that she wore unusual clothes and had an unusual hairstyle. But what's wrong with that?

I guess it especially bothered me because it reminded me of the kids in Horace's class teasing him. But I didn't say anything. The last thing I wanted to do was to get into an argument with Jenny Carlin.

When Hope came into the classroom after lunch, Jenny called out, "Hey, what did you have for lunch, Hope?"

Hope looked at her, confused. "Why do you want to know?"

"I was just wondering if it was anything that I've ever heard of," Jenny said.

A hurt look spread across Hope's face. She

turned and walked to her desk and sat down without another word.

"Why don't you mind your own business," Kate told Jenny.

Jenny folded her arms across her chest. "At least I don't dress like a hippie!" she said loudly enough for Hope to hear.

"Cut it out," I told Jenny. It was bad enough to talk about Hope, but it was even worse to say it right in front of her. "I'm going to go talk to her," I told the others. I wanted her to know that *we* weren't mean like Jenny and Angela.

I walked over to Hope's desk and Stephanie followed me. "Don't pay any attention to her," I said, smiling. "She's like that to everyone."

"Yeah, she won the Miss Rude Award at the beginning of the year," Stephanie added.

Hope smiled weakly. "It's okay."

"So, I guess you're coming to the party!" Stephanie said excitedly. "It's going to be a lot of fun. We're going to pick people to work on the decorations this afternoon, if you're interested. Since you're so good at art, I hope you'll help." Stephanie wrinkled her nose. "Otherwise I might end up working with Jenny and Angela!"

Hope shrugged. "I don't know. I'll have to see. I might be busy."

Then the bell rang and Stephanie and I started back to our desks.

"She *really* doesn't want to be here," Stephanie whispered to me. "I don't think I've ever been so nice to someone so cold in my life. Do you still think she's just shy?"

"I don't know," I said truthfully. I know a lot about shyness. When someone's nice to me, I don't usually feel so shy anymore. I mean, it's really hard for me to go up to someone and start talking. But if someone comes up to *me*, then it's not so difficult. I just don't like making the first move.

No, it was pretty clear that Hope was more than just shy. I thought Stephanie was right: for some reason Hope didn't want to be in our class. But why? "Maybe she really misses her old school," I said. "It's hard to move — *we* both know that."

"Yeah, but it makes it ten times harder if you don't try to make friends at your new school," Stephanie said.

As I slid into my seat, I wondered where Hope came from. Maybe she was far away from her old friends. Maybe she would never see them again. I knew I wouldn't be able to stand it if I had to move a long way from Lauren, Stephanie, and Kate. I crossed my fingers and hoped that would never happen!

* * *

At the end of the day there was a quick discussion of the party. "I see that several people have signed up to bring refreshments already," said Mrs. Mead. "Terrific! Now, who would like to assist Stephanie on the decorations committee? First of all, let me say that you must be free Tuesday and Thursday afternoons, because those are the times the art studio and gym will be free for you to work."

That did it for me — the Quarks club meets every Tuesday afternoon, and I couldn't miss that. Lauren and Kate raised their hands right away.

"A few more people would be great," Stephanie said. "There's a lot of work to do."

"How about some boys?" Mrs. Mead asked.

Pete Stone slowly raised his hand. Then, to my surprise, Henry said, "okay, I'll help. But don't make me cut out any hearts."

I wished I could give up the Quarks just for the next few weeks. Everyone was going to have so much fun working on the decorations . . . and working with Henry would be great.

Mrs. Mead jotted down names. Then she looked around the room. "We need one more volunteer. Hope, what about you? This would be a good opportunity to meet people," she said warmly.

Stephanie looked toward her eagerly.

35

Hope shook her head. "Sorry, I can't on Tuesday afternoons — I'm joining the Quarks Club."

Kate looked around at me, surprised. I shrugged, to show that I was surprised by Hope's announcement, too.

"Oh, well, that sounds like a good idea," said Mrs. Mead. "Anyone else?"

Karla Stamos raised her hand. "I'd like to help," she said.

I smiled. I knew Stephanie was groaning inside. She had worked with Karla before, on the class newspaper, and she hadn't liked it.

The bell rang and everyone scrambled out of their seats. I wanted to get home early and find out how Horace's day had gone.

"So is our first meeting tomorrow?" Kate asked Stephanie as we walked down the hall toward the front door.

"Yep," Stephanie said. "Kate, guess what? Mrs. Mead wants me to get someone to be vice-chairperson, you know, to help me out. And in case I get sick or something, that person could take over."

"Yeah? So who are you going to ask? No, don't tell me — Karla, right?" Kate grinned.

"No, you!"

"Oh." Kate seemed to be thinking it over. "Let me check my datebook and I'll get back to you."

"Are you serious?" Stephanie said, her eyes wide. "You have to help me! You have to make all the lists!"

Kate broke up laughing. "Well . . . okay," she said.

Lauren stuck her nose up in the air. "I want you to know that I am extremely offended you didn't ask me," she told Stephanie.

"Give me a break!" Kate moaned. "If Lauren were in charge of organizing things, we'd end up having the party *next* Valentine's Day!"

Lauren giggled. "Well, maybe I could get it going by the Fourth of July." We headed over to the bicycle rack and climbed onto our bikes. We ride to school in the winter as long as it's not *too* snowy or icy.

"Patti, I almost forgot — can you believe that Hope is joining the Quarks?" Stephanie shook her head. "I didn't think she was going to get involved with anything at school."

"I know. She still sits by herself at lunch every day," Lauren added. "I made a joke the other day when I bumped into her at the water fountain and she didn't even laugh!"

Kate shook her head. "Imagine that."

"I noticed that she's really smart in science," I said. "I was kind of hoping she'd join the club. We can always use new members."

"That is, *if* she says anything at the meetings!" Stephanie added.

"Don't you see — this is the perfect opportunity for us to find out why she's so quiet all the time!" Kate exclaimed as we turned the corner.

"Yeah, Patti — you have to talk to her some more," Stephanie urged me.

"Well, I'll try," I said. "But she hasn't been very friendly so far. And I don't want to pressure her."

"Who said anything about pressuring her?" Kate said innocently.

I shifted gears as we coasted down the hill. Kate didn't think anything of bluntly asking people questions about their life, but it wasn't exactly my style.

Anyway, I was more concerned about Horace, who still wanted to quit school. My mother had to coax him out the door that morning. But I wasn't about to let him drop out of school, just because some stupid kids were making fun of him. It wasn't his fault he was smart — or that he was shorter than his classmates. Pretty soon he'd start growing tall just like me, and then those kids would be sorry they teased him!

And in the meantime, I'd fight those bullies myself if they didn't leave him alone!

Chapter 5

"So what did you find out?" Kate asked me eagerly on Wednesday morning when we met to ride to school.

I didn't have to ask what she was talking about — lately Kate had become obsessed with discovering what Hope's story was. When she makes up her mind about something, nothing stops her. "Not much," I admitted. "She's from California."

"Wow — California," Stephanie breathed. "I've always wanted to live there." Stephanie's hooked on movie stars — one in particular, Kevin DeSpain — and says she's going to become a Hollywood actress herself some day. Either that or a fashion designer.

"I think that's why she's being so quiet. She's a

long way from all her old friends," I said. "I get the feeling she's lonely here."

"Well, that explains why she wears those clothes," said Kate. "Everyone in California does."

"Not everyone," I said. "That's just a stereotype."

"I wonder if she knows how to surf," Lauren mused. "Wouldn't it be cool if she did?"

"Maybe she lived in L.A. and got to see some movie stars — better yet, maybe she lived in Beverly Hills! Can you imagine, shopping on Rodeo Drive instead of at the Riverhurst Mall?" Stephanie shook her head. "Talk about heaven!"

"There's only one way to find out," Kate said in a determined voice. "We'll just have to keep trying to get to know her."

"Whether she wants to know us or not," Lauren muttered to me.

When we arrived at school, Kate marched right up to Hope's desk. "Hi!" she said cheerfully. "How's it going?"

"Fine," Hope replied. She was busy unpacking her knapsack.

"Patti tells me you're from California," Kate went on.

Hope nodded. "That's right, I am."

"I'd love to hear about it," Kate said. "How about going for ice cream after school? And maybe my friends can come, too."

"Thanks for offering," Hope answered. "But, I don't eat ice cream."

Kate looked like she was going to fall over.

"Not eat ice cream?" Lauren whispered in my ear. "What's wrong with her?"

"Well, it doesn't have to be ice cream," Kate continued. "We can get something else."

"I'm sorry, but I can't," said Hope.

Kate folded her arms across her chest. She had her famous "I'm not going to give up!" expression on her face. "The Quarks Club doesn't meet today, you know," she told Hope.

"I have a lot of homework," Hope explained. "Since I transferred in the middle of the term and everything."

"Oh." Kate tapped her foot against the floor. "Well, all right," she said. Then she turned and walked back to her desk.

"You didn't have to give her the third degree," Lauren told Kate when she slid into the seat next to her.

"You were grilling her like she was a criminal," Stephanie added.

"No, I wasn't. I was trying to be nice to her!"

41

Kate fumed. "She's hiding something, I know it. I bet you she's not even from California — she probably just said that to throw us off the track," Kate remarked.

"What are you, a private investigator?" Lauren scoffed.

"I know — maybe she's a princess," Stephanie said mysteriously, "like your neighbor, Lauren."

We all started laughing. When Lauren was moving into her new house not too long ago, Stephanie made up a story about the next-door neighbor to keep Lauren's mind off leaving her old house.

"Not that again!" Lauren whispered back. "She's just a kid like the rest of us."

"Except that she doesn't like ice cream," Stephanie added.

Lauren made a face. "On second thought, we have absolutely nothing in common!"

After school I got my bike and headed around the building to Horace's classroom to pick him up. Usually my mom does it, or he gets a ride home with one of his friends' mothers. But I was still worried about him and I wanted to make sure he was okay. That morning he had pretended to be sick so he didn't have to go to school. My mother and father saw right through it, though. Horace doesn't usually lie, so I knew the situation at school hadn't improved.

Whan I got there, I could hardly believe my eyes. Horace was sitting outside on the steps, and a bunch of kids were hanging around him, talking and laughing. *Maybe Horace finally made some friends!* I thought happily.

I put my bike down on the ground and walked up to the steps with a smile on my face. Then I heard what they were saying.

"Are you waiting for your *mommy* to pick you up?" one boy said.

"What's the matter? Can't you make it home by yourself?" another one taunted him. "Or would you get *lost*?"

"Mr. Genius here probably doesn't even know how to ride a bike yet!" another added with a loud laugh.

"I do so!" Horace shouted. His face was bright red and he looked like he was about to start crying!

I marched up to the group. "He does too know how to ride a bike," I said.

"Yeah — with training wheels!" the first boy said.

"Why don't you leave him alone," I said angrily. "Come on, Horace, let's go."

"What are you, his *girlfriend*?" one of the boys asked.

"No, I'm his sister! And you'd better stop making fun of him! He can't help it if he's smarter than you are!" I practically yelled. I was so mad at those little shrimps!

Meanwhile, Horace had gotten up and was walking down the sidewalk.

"Maybe I'm not a genius, but I don't need my big sister to protect me!" one of them yelled as I grabbed my bike and hurried after Horace. He was walking so fast, he had already turned the corner onto the next street.

"Wait up!" I called out. He kept walking and didn't turn around. When I caught up to him, he didn't even look at me.

"Those guys are real jerks," I said sympathetically. "But you know, they're just jealous of you."

Horace didn't say anything.

"Hey, you want to stop off at Sweet Stuff on the way home?" I asked him. Horace loves their cookies more than anything.

"No," Horace said.

"Why not? Aren't you hungry?" I asked.

"I don't want to do anything with you!" he suddenly blurted out.

I stopped walking. "What? Why not?"

"You shouldn't have come over to pick me up,"

Horace said angrily. "And you shouldn't have told those guys to leave me alone!"

"I — I was just t-trying to help," I stammered. Horace had never yelled at me before!

"You made me look like a baby," he said. "Now they have even *more* to tease me about. No one else's sister comes to their class to pick them up. Don't ever do it again!" Horace said. He started walking down the sidewalk at top speed again.

I followed him the rest of the way home, too stunned to do anything else. Horace was furious with me! I guess I shouldn't have tried to help him, but what was I supposed to do? Stand there and listen while a bunch of mean kids made fun of him?

"It was awful," I told everybody the next day at lunch. "I completely embarrassed Horace, and now he won't even talk to me!"

I twirled my fork around on my plate. Normally the cafeteria's spaghetti is pretty good, but I just wasn't in the mood for it that day. To tell you the truth, I hadn't been hungry since Horace yelled at me.

"You could call the other kids' parents and tell them to tell their kids to cut it out," Lauren suggested. "They'd never find out who did it."

"No, that wouldn't work," I said, shaking my head. "Then everyone would know Horace had told on them, and they'd hate him."

"What if he just teases them right back?" asked Kate. "You could give him some really good lines to use."

"No, Horace can already think of his own lines. He's just afraid to say them." I twisted my watch around my wrist.

"If you ask me," said Stephanie, "the best thing to do is try not to think about it."

I stared at her. "What do you mean?"

Stephanie dabbed the corners of her mouth with a napkin. "Well, it's obvious that you can't do anything about it. It's Horace's problem, and if he doesn't want you to help him, you can't. The way I see it, Horace has to come up with his own way to fight back. Otherwise those kids will have even more to tease him about."

I nodded. "Yeah, I definitely made a mistake yesterday with the big sister routine."

"Think about it — Horace is the smartest little kid we know," Stephanie went on.

"Except Melissa," Kate interjected. Melissa's her little sister.

We all smiled.

"Well, anyway, he's bound to think of something sooner or later," Stephanie predicted. "Didn't he come up with a way to rig up Adelaide's bowl so that the cat food automatically dropped into it every morning?"

I laughed. "Yeah."

Stephanie waved her hand in the air. "Piece of cake!"

"What kind?" joked Lauren, glancing over her shoulder at the lunchline.

I smiled and took a big bite of spaghetti. It was a little cold, but it still tasted good. I was glad I had such good friends. They made everything seem better — even cafeteria food.

Chapter 6

"Ta-da!" Lauren spun around in a circle. "Instant greaser!" She was wearing baggy jeans rolled up at the bottom, a white T-shirt, and her brother Roger's jean jacket, which is about eight sizes too big for her. She had her father's sunglasses on, too.

Kate shook her head. "You look like you should be in a motorcycle gang."

It was Friday night and we were at Lauren's house, trying on outfits for the dance. We only had a week to find something to wear — and to learn how to dance fifties-style.

"I kind of like it," Stephanie said. "But maybe we should find something else, too, in case you decide you'd rather look like a girl." She rummaged in Lauren's closet. "Only I can't *find* anything in here!" she complained.

"I'm shocked," Kate said, rolling her eyes. Lauren is notorious for being messy.

Stephanie snapped her fingers. "I know — you can borrow one of your mom's cardigan sweaters. Does she have a pink one? That would be perfect."

"I'll go ask," Lauren said. But when she turned to walk out the door, she banged into the wall.

"Yeah, those sunglasses will be great at the party!" Kate teased her. "You can bump into everyone while you're dancing."

Lauren slid the glasses down her nose and frowned at Kate. "At least I'll *look* cool," she said.

"Okay Patti, you're next," Stephanie declared. She pulled a skirt out of her overnight bag and shook it a few times. It was a poodle skirt — just like the one I'd worn on the float — only it was hot pink instead of yellow, and it had a huge "P" stitched into it.

"Where did you get that?" I asked, amazed.

"Clothing Classics," Stephanie said. "I found it in the sale bin. Isn't it cool?"

Dressing up for a party or a parade was one thing, but I didn't know if I would have the nerve to wear a skirt like that to *school* — especially in that color. "Do you think the 'P' is overdoing it a little, maybe?" I asked hesitantly. I didn't want to hurt Stephanie's feelings, but I wasn't sure I was ready to make such a bold fashion statement!

"Not at all," Stephanie said. "You can wear a plain white blouse to tone it down a little, if you want, and white sneakers with pink bobby socks."

"Kate, what do you think?" I asked. Kate isn't an authority on clothes like Stephanie, but she is sensible, and common sense was definitely required in this situation!

Kate looked up from the magazine she was reading. "It's okay. Actually, if you curl your hair, you'll look just like those girls in *Grease*."

"I think you could get second place in the costume contest with this skirt," Stephanie declared. "After me, natch."

"What are *you* wearing, anyway?" Kate asked. "You haven't shown us yet."

Stephanie shook her head. "And I'm not going to, either. You'll just have to come to the party to find out — if you can stand the suspense."

"Oh, puh-leeze!" Kate sighed.

Lauren reappeared in the doorway holding a bag of barbecue potato chips and a bowl of sour-cream dip. A six-pack of soda was draped over her arm.

"I thought you were going to get the sweater," Stephanie said.

Lauren shrugged and set the food down on the floor. "I got sidetracked."

50

"I'm glad you did," I said. "I was getting kind of hungry!"

Everyone dug into the chips and started munching away.

"What food are you all bringing to the party?" Lauren asked.

"It figures you'd want to know that," Kate said. "I'm making my marshmallow super-fudge — oh, that reminds me! I forgot to tell you guys. After school I ran back into the classroom to get my datebook, and Hope was in there."

"So?" Lauren said.

"So, Hope was telling Mrs. Mead that she didn't think her father would be able to come after all." Kate took another handful of chips.

"You're kidding!" Stephanie exclaimed.

"Do you think *she* decided not to come, too?" I asked, scooping some dip onto a chip. "That would be too bad."

"Maybe Jenny's teasing got to her," Lauren said. "Or maybe she really is embarrassed about her dad or something."

"That's crazy!" Stephanie said. I didn't really understand either.

"Or maybe Hope just chickened out." Kate took a soda from the six-pack and popped it open.

"Why would she do that?" I asked.

"I still think she's hiding *something*. Every time we try to talk to her she just clams up," Kate said.

"What's she supposed to do — give a book report on her life?" Lauren asked.

"No . . . but she looks so unhappy all the time, and she never talks to anyone," Kate pointed out. "I just don't get it."

"Well, I think she's just homesick," I said.

"But she's been here practically two weeks already!" Kate argued.

"Look, Kate, you've lived here all your life," Stephanie reminded her. "You don't know what it's like to move, especially all the way across the country."

"Stephanie's right," I said. "Maybe she's always lived in California. If you moved away from here, you'd still miss it after two weeks, wouldn't you?"

"I guess," Kate admitted.

"You *guess*?" Lauren reached over and started tickling Kate's feet. "Thanks a lot!"

"Okay, okay — I'd probably never get over it!" Kate gasped in between laughs. "Anyway, I have a plan."

Lauren grimaced. "Uh-oh. Here we go."

"Well, we want to find out more about her, right? And she never wants to do anything after school. We can solve both questions by following her home one afternoon," Kate announced.

"Really, Kate, you should give her some privacy," I said. "She'll tell us more about herself when she's ready. We don't have to know every little detail about her, anyway!" I knew I sounded a little angry, but Kate was going too far. If Hope wanted to be alone, it wasn't right for us to bombard her with questions and start spying on her. Stephanie and Lauren both nodded, agreeing with me.

"I still think it's a good idea," Kate said with a frown. She doesn't like it when people disagree with her. She's used to being right!

"Let's listen to that *Hits from the Fifties* tape Patti brought and practice hopping in our socks," Lauren suggested, smoothly changing the subject. She stood up and brushed a few crumbs off her jeans. "Okay, first we have to learn to do the jitterbug."

She reached over to her cassette player and was about to press the play button when Stephanie said, "Wait a second, Lauren. Did you guys just hear that?"

"Hear what?" I said.

Then I heard it — the howling. It sounded like a pack of wolves was standing outside the Hunters' house!

"Sounds like we have visitors," Stephanie said, smiling.

53

Lauren walked over to the window and pulled the curtain back. She lifted the shade and looked outside. "It's three boys, but I can't make out their faces!" She opened the window a crack. "Who's out there?" she yelled.

"The Werewolf!" Larry Jackson answered. I recognized his voice.

"And the Big Bad Wolf!" added Henry. I grinned.

"And Wolfman Jack!" Willie Judd chimed in. Willie is Larry's cousin, and one of the cutest boys in sixth grade. He lives just up the street from Lauren. The three of them started howling again.

"We're here to challenge you to the first annual February snowball fight!" Henry yelled up to the window. We'd had another snowstorm that day, so the snow was all fresh — and deep.

"We accept!" Lauren answered. She shut the window with a bang. "Come on, troops, let's go. We're going to nail those guys!"

We practically flew downstairs. I pulled on my boots as fast I could, then wrapped a scarf around my neck and got into my ski jacket. When we were all ready, Lauren threw open the door and shouted, "Charge!" A snowball hit her right in the stomach. "This means war!" she yelled.

I quickly crouched down behind a bush and

made four or five snowballs. In front of me, Kate and Stephanie were making snowballs and throwing them as fast as they could at Larry and Willie, who were firing their own right back. Stephanie was shrieking, and Kate was trying to tell her how to make the perfect snowball. Lauren was creeping around the side of the house to get a better shot at them. I didn't see Henry anywhere. I figured he was planning a sneak attack.

"Oh, Patti!" he called out a minute later in a singsong voice. "Where are you?"

I looked up and saw him walking around the corner of the house. I watched him carefully. When he looked the other way to toss a snowball at Lauren, I stood up and hurled my biggest one. It hit him on the shoulder.

He whirled around, laughing. "I'll get you for that, Jenkins!" he threatened.

Suddenly the Hunters' front door opened and Mr. Hunter stepped outside. "What's going on here?" he asked. "Lauren?"

Instead of answering, Lauren tossed a snowball at him. It hit him on the knee and crumpled at his feet. "Oh, I see," he said with a chuckle. "That's what's going on."

Mr. Hunter was about to make his own snowball when Bullwinkle, their dog, bounded out the front door past him. Bullwinkle is a *big* dog. He's very friendly, but when he jumps up on you to say hello he can knock you right over!

For some reason, Bullwinkle headed straight for Henry, who was in the middle of throwing his next bomb at me. Bullwinkle jumped up in the air and tried to catch the snowball in his teeth. Instead the snow just broke into pieces and fell to the ground.

"Hey, no fair!" Henry complained. "That makes it five against three."

"What's the matter — is the Big Bad Wolf afraid of a little dog?" Lauren teased him.

"All right, Hunter, you asked for this," Henry said. He started running toward her.

But Bullwinkle is very loyal to Lauren. He ran up to Henry and tackled him!

We all started laughing. "The girls win!" Kate cried.

"It's a knockout!" Lauren added.

Henry stood up, covered with snow from head to toe. Even his face was all white. "Ha-ha, very funny," he said, brushing the snow off.

"Why don't you all come in for some hot chocolate?" Mr. Hunter offered from the doorway.

"All right!" Pete started hurrying toward the house and Willie followed him.

I began making my way through the snow when

Stephanie whispered, "Hey — look over there!" She pointed across the street. "It's Hope."

I looked across the street. Sure enough, there was a girl with long blonde hair about Hope's height standing under the streetlight.

"You're right!" Kate said. "Maybe she lives on your street, Lauren!"

"Should I ask her if she wants to come over?" Lauren asked.

"Definitely!" Kate said. Then she yelled, "Hope! Hope! It's me, Kate Beekman! Hi!"

Hope didn't answer. "Maybe it's just someone who looks like Hope," I said.

Stephanie stared at me. "No one else looks like her," she said.

"Hope, we're going inside for some hot chocolate!" Lauren yelled. "Why don't you come over?"

But suddenly, the girl standing under the streetlight was gone. "She vanished!" Lauren said softly.

"I told you she never wants to do anything with us!" Kate said smugly. "Did you see the way she was standing there, just watching us in the dark? Tell me there isn't something weird about that!"

"Let's go inside," Lauren said. "The hot chocolate should be ready by now."

As Kate followed Lauren inside, I heard her say, "So, she must live on your street."

"You don't know that for sure," Lauren argued. "You don't even know if that girl was Hope!"

"There's only one way to find out," Kate insisted. "And that's by following her!"

Kate wasn't about to give up on her plan to play detective. I heaved a loud sigh and turned to go up the front walk. To my surprise, I saw that Henry was still standing on the front lawn.

"Aren't you coming in?" I asked him.

"No, I'm protesting," he said with a frown. "That was not a fair fight."

"If I know Lauren, there are lots of marshmallows in the hot chocolate," I said. "And I think there may be some cookies lying around." I didn't want Henry to go home mad! Besides, I liked the idea of hanging out with him on a Friday night.

"Well . . . okay," he finally agreed. "But only if the dog stays out!"

Later that night, Lauren was reaching up to turn off the light. "Sweet dreams! Especially you, Patti!"

I rolled over and fluffed my pillow. "What do you mean?"

"You and Henry, natch!" Lauren said, giggling.

"Shh!" I whispered. I didn't want the whole neighborhood to know I liked him!

"Are you going to give Henry a valentine?" Stephanie wanted to know.

"I don't think so," I said. It was one thing to like him, but it was another to let him know I did. I'd die of embarrassment if he found out — and even worse if his friends did.

"Oh, come on. You have to," Stephanie urged me.

"Yeah, get into the spirit of the holiday," Lauren said.

"I don't see you guys making any valentines for the boys you like," I pointed out.

"I might," Stephanie said. She yawned.

"What about you, Kate?" asked Lauren.

"No way!" Kate turned over in her sleeping bag. "First of all, there aren't any boys I like enough to make a valentine for. Second of all, if I did send one, I sure wouldn't sign my name!"

"Yeah, you'd probably sign my name instead," Lauren said with a laugh.

Usually I just give valentines to my friends and my family. The thought of giving one to a boy I liked was scary. What if he crumpled it up? Not that I thought Henry would . . . but he might think I liked him *too* much. I sighed. It was all so difficult.

"Hey, I have an idea," Kate said.

"Uh-oh," Lauren said. "Another idea."

"Maybe we could all get together to make some valentines this week — you know, give each other ideas and stuff," said Kate. "We can do it at my house, in the basement — we have all those art supplies down there."

"That sounds like a good idea," I said. "When should we do it?"

"Well, we're going to be pretty busy with the decorations." Kate paused for a minute. "How about if we do it Thursday night over dinner? We can get a pizza and finish the cards by seven — that'll give us plenty of time to do our homework, too."

"Great idea!" Lauren said. "How does that sound, Stephanie?"

Instead of answering, Stephanie snored lightly — just once, but it was hysterical.

Lauren giggled. "It sounds like she agrees!"

"Mrmhmphf," was all Stephanie had to say.

Chapter 7

By Sunday night, Horace was talking to me again. I don't know why. I don't think he had forgiven me yet for "butting in," as he called it, but he seemed willing to forget about it anyway. First-graders — whoops, I mean second-graders — can be that way.

According to my mom, the kids at school were still bugging him. Horace wasn't talking about it, though. My parents said it was time for them to have a talk with his teacher, but I convinced them to wait a little while longer. Horace was so sensitive about other people helping him — I knew from firsthand experience — and I didn't want us to make things worse for him at school. I wished there was *something* I could do, though.

On Monday, we practically had to restrain Kate to keep her from rushing over to Hope the second she walked into the classroom. I told Kate to give Hope a few more days before she set out to play detective. She agreed, but she said she was only going to wait until the end of the week. Then, if we still didn't know why Hope was so quiet, Kate was going to start her investigation (she actually called it that!).

It was funny, because as soon as we sat down to start class, I noticed a change in Hope. When Henry made a joke, she actually laughed along with the rest of us. She smiled a few other times, too, and when we had to break into pairs and work together, she and Karla seemed to get along okay.

When the bell rang for lunch, Hope seemed as eager as everyone else to get out of the classroom and head for the cafeteria. In the past, she had dawdled behind, almost as if she dreaded it. I can understand that feeling. Not knowing who you're going to sit with — or if you're going to sit with anybody — is a real drag.

Anyway, I thought she might sit with us, but instead she sat with Karla. Karla wasn't the most interesting person in our class, but at least Hope was sitting with *someone*! It was almost as if Hope had heard Kate saying she had until the end of the week to be sociable!

"I'm going to get some more chocolate milk,"

Lauren said, standing up. "Does anyone want anything?"

"No, thanks," I said.

"If they have any french fries, bring some back," Stephanie said.

As I ate my grilled cheese sandwich, I watched Lauren in the lunchline. Suddenly Hope was at her side. It looked like she was getting more milk, too.

"I can't believe it!" Kate said. "Hope and Lauren are actually having a conversation."

She was right — both of them had gotten their cartons of milk, and they were standing off to one side of the line. Then Lauren nodded and walked back to our table.

"What did you do? What did you say?" Kate demanded.

Lauren laughed. "Don't have a cow! I just asked her if she lived in my neighborhood, and she said she lives on Birch Street, only a few blocks from Brio Drive."

"So was that her on Friday night?" asked Stephanie.

"Yeah. She said she was out walking her dog, and she thought it was us, but then she saw Bullwinkle and decided she should probably get going." Lauren shrugged. "I guess her dog is a little smaller."

"Even a *bear* is smaller than Bullwinkle!" I said.

63

"It's great that you live so close to her. Maybe we'll see her around more. And now you don't have to follow her," I told Kate.

Kate looked disappointed. She had been all excited about the thrill of the chase.

"I asked her why she always brought her own lunch, too," Lauren said. "She said it seems like no one around here likes the food she likes. I asked her what kind of food that was, and she told me she's a vegetarian!"

"Did you tell her you're a choco-tarian?" Stephanie asked Lauren.

Lauren grinned. "Well, I sort of said that I didn't like vegetables, but that lots of other people probably did. Anyhow, I told her she should come to the party even if she doesn't like the food we have," Lauren shrugged. "I don't know if she will, though."

Tuesday afternoon I went to my Quarks Club meeting. "I have to leave early today," Hope said as she sat down next to me. "Will you tell me when it's ten to four? I forgot my watch. I kind of spaced out today."

That was the longest thing I had ever heard her say! "Sure, I'll let you know," I said.

"If you're a little spacey you'll fit right into this club," said Todd Farrell, who was sitting across from

64

us. "I'm going to be an astronaut, myself. I plan to be on the first mission to establish life stations on Saturn."

"You've been watching too many *Star Trek* reruns," Betsy Chalfin said, shaking her head. Hope and I laughed.

Our adviser, Mr. Murdock, walked into the room and put down his briefcase. "Ready to save the planet?" he asked us.

"Ready!" a couple of kids answered. We'd been working on a big project to clean up the environment. Not the whole environment, but our little piece of it in Riverhurst. That week we were starting a campaign to try to stop restaurants from using certain kinds of plastic — the kinds that don't disintegrate ever, or at least take hundreds and hundreds of years to do so.

At ten to four I leaned over to Hope and pointed to my watch. "It's time for you to go," I whispered. Todd and Betsy were in the middle of a big argument about the best way to get rid of garbage.

"Thanks," she said softly. She picked up her flowered knapsack and slunk quietly out of the room.

Horace was going to meet me just inside the front doors of the school at four, when the Quarks let out. He wanted to make absolutely sure that I wouldn't show up at *his* class again.

As I walked down the empty hallway, I thought

I heard Horace talking to somebody. Suddenly I rec-ognized the other voice. It was Hope's! I slowed down and peeked around the corner to the front entrance. I couldn't believe it! Hope and Horace were sitting side by side on one of the benches.

"So why don't you like your new school?" Hope was asking him.

"It's not a new school," Horace said, "it's a new class."

"Oh," Hope said. "Well, what's wrong with it?"

"The kids are mean to me. They make fun of me because I skipped a grade. They say I'm too little, and I'm too smart. They hate me," Horace com-plained.

"They probably don't *hate* you," Hope said. "But I know what you mean. I just moved into a new class, too, and I don't like it very much, either."

"Do they make fun of you, too?" Horace asked.

"Some of them do," Hope admitted with a shrug. "Not because I'm smart but because I'm dif-ferent. They think my clothes are funny and the foods I eat are weird, too. But some of the kids are nice. Aren't some of the kids in your class nice to you?"

"I guess," Horace shrugged.

"Don't worry about the other ones, then," Hope advised. "If they're too dumb to realize what a great person you are, you don't want them to be your friends, anyway, right? And don't get upset when they tell you you're weird. There's nothing wrong with being different." She laughed. "At least I hope not!"

Even Horace started to giggle, and I hadn't heard him laugh in about a week. I was amazed — Hope had done more good talking to Horace than I had. She was really good with him. I wondered if she had a little brother or sister.

While they were still laughing, I stepped around the corner. "Horace! Sorry it took me so long," I said. "Hi, Hope."

"Hi," she said shyly.

"I thought you had to leave early for something . . . ." I said. I wasn't trying to pry, but I guess it came out sounding that way.

"My dad's supposed to pick me up, but he's not here yet," she said. "Wait a minute — is Horace your brother?"

I nodded.

"Oh!" She laughed. "He said he was waiting for Patti, but I didn't know it was *you*."

"It's me," I said nervously. "Um, Horace, how was school today?"

"Rotten," he said, pushing his glasses up on his nose. "But I don't care — it's okay to be weird!" He smiled at Hope.

"That's right, we're in the Weirdo Club," Hope told him.

"I'm going to get a drink of water," Horace announced. He slid off the bench and dashed down the hall.

"So," I said. "I, uh, heard you talking to Horace about how the kids tease him. It's really been worrying me. Do you have any idea how he can get them to stop?" I asked her.

"Well . . . there is one thing that seems to work," she said. "At least it did for me once. Kids tease you because they want you to get mad, right? If you don't, then there's no point in teasing you."

"Right," I said. "And Horace always gets upset and tries to answer them back. His face and ears turn all red," I explained. "Then they make fun of *that*."

"Hm." Hope twisted one of her tiny braids around her finger. "What if he just *agrees* with everything they say?"

"What do you mean?"

"If they say he's a genius, he should just say, 'You're right, I am.' And if they say he's a shrimp, he can say, 'You're right.' That way it'll be really obvious that what they're saying doesn't bother him."

"That's a great idea," I said. "Thanks."

A car pulled up outside and honked, and Hope

jumped up. "That's my dad — gotta go," she said. "See you tomorrow!" Then she dashed down the front steps and hopped into the car.

I stood there for a minute, realizing that there was a lot more to Hope Lenski than I had thought. She was smart, caring, and funny, too. I didn't know her that well yet, but what I knew, I liked! And if her plan for Horace worked, I would like her even more! She had already helped by telling him it was okay to be different from other people.

The next day, I decided to ask Hope if she wanted to do something after school. But I wasn't going to tell Lauren or Stephanie — and especially not Kate — about it. I had a feeling Hope would be scared off if we all went along. It's hard to get to know somebody when there's a whole group of people. And Kate would probably ask her every question in the book.

This was one of those times when I *had* to keep a secret from my friends. I told myself it was for a good cause.

Right after lunch I followed Hope back to the classroom. "Hope?" I said, walking just behind her.

She stopped and I practically bumped into her.

"Oops — sorry," I said.

"Hi, Patti," she said.

"I was, um, wondering if you wanted to do something after school today. You know, if you have time."

"Well, I have a dentist's appointment today — But maybe tomorrow?" Hope said. "What do you want to do?"

"I don't know. Maybe we could go somewhere for a soda — or fruit juice," I quickly added. I didn't know if vegetarians liked Dr Pepper.

"You know what I could really go for?" Hope asked. "Some frozen yogurt."

"There's a place called Sweet Stuff that has ice cream, frozen yogurt, and cookies," I said.

"Sure," said Hope. "That sounds good."

Then I remembered that Kate, Lauren, and Stephanie had a meeting of the decorations committee on Thursday afternoon. I smiled as I walked back into the classroom. Talk about a perfect plan! I wouldn't even have to lie.

Chapter 8

"I'll have a vanilla Tofutti with nuts and raisins on top," Hope told the girl behind the counter the following afternoon.

"And I'll, um, have a raspberry Tofutti," I said. Normally my favorite is buttercrunch ice cream — with toffee chips mixed in — but I thought I'd try something new. I didn't want to make Hope feel funny.

We got our dishes and walked over to a small table. "I like this place," Hope said when we sat down. She licked her spoon. "Good Tofutti! It's even better than frozen yogurt!"

"Yeah, we hang out here a lot," I said. I took a bite of my own. It wasn't too bad. I wasn't about to convert to being a Tofutti lover overnight, though.

"Do you and your friends — Stephanie and Kate

71

and Lauren — do everything together?" Hope asked.

"Well . . . not everything," I said. "But a lot of things. We do different stuff after school — you know, like I'm in the Quarks Club and they're not. And Kate's in the Video Club. Lauren likes sports, and Stephanie, well, she likes a lot of different stuff." I smiled. I was supposed to be finding out more about Hope, not telling her all about the Sleepover Friends! "Did you have a group of best friends like that back home in California?" I asked.

Hope shrugged. "I had one best friend, actually. I miss her a lot."

"I bet," I said, nodding. "You know, I just moved here not too long ago."

"Really?" Hope's eyes lit up. "So I'm not the only new kid in town?"

"Nope, not by a long shot." I took a big bite of Tofutti. The more I ate it, the more I liked it. Hope was on to something good with this stuff. "Stephanie only moved here a little while before I did. And a couple of other kids in our class are new, too."

Hope sighed. "That makes me feel better. I hate feeling like everyone else knows what's going on, when I don't."

"It's tough moving to a new school," I agreed. "I remember how much I hated it at first."

"Everything here is just so different from back home," Hope said.

"Really?" That surprised me. Aren't kids the same everywhere?

"Sure," Hope said, flipping her hair over one shoulder. She had taken the braids out, and it was all kinky. "I mean, at lunchtime, even in the winter, we all used to go outside." She laughed. "You sure can't do that here."

"Well, the weather's different here, that's true," I said. "I'd love to go to California — I've never been there."

"It's great," Hope said dreamily.

"Why did you move?" I asked. I didn't mean to be so blunt, but the question just slipped out.

Hope seemed sort of flustered. She took a bite of Tofutti and let it melt in her mouth before she answered. "Uh, my dad wanted to move back here because he grew up in Riverhurst. He has a lot of friends here. And we were getting tired of living in a big city, with all the hassles and how expensive everything is, you know."

I nodded. My parents had moved to Riverhurst for some of the same reasons. "Do you have any brothers or sisters?" I asked.

"I have a little brother who's five," she said.

73

"You're probably not going to believe this, but his name is Rain," she said, smiling.

"As in the stuff that comes out of clouds?"

She nodded and blushed. "My parents kind of went crazy when they named us."

"Mine, too!" I said. "They named me Patricia, and then there's *Horace*." I shook my head. "They should have bought one of those books with ten thousand baby names. Actually, I like the name Patti. It's just the Patricia I don't like."

"I guess I like my name, too," said Hope. "Even though some people think it's weird."

"I don't!" I said. "I think it's nice. I never knew anyone named Hope before." And I never knew anyone *like* Hope before, I was thinking. "Hey, speaking of parents, I have to call home to tell my mom I'm going to be late. Do you want to call your mom, too?"

Hope frowned and tossed her empty paper cup in the trash. "No, I'll call my Dad, though."

"Oh, does your mom work full time?" I asked.

"Sort of," Hope mumbled. "She's not home. I mean, she's hard to reach when she's at the office. Since my dad works at home, he's the one who's expecting me," she added quickly.

"What does he do?" I asked.

"He's a veterinarian."

"Wow! How cool!" I said. "Do you get to see lots of cute animals? I love animals — all kinds," I said.

"Even snakes?" Hope asked with a grin.

"Does he really treat snakes?" I asked.

"Sure," Hope said. "Lots of people keep them for pets. Mostly he sees dogs, cats, and birds — and sometimes he goes to farms to treat horses and cows."

"That must be so neat, getting to look at all the animals," I said. "I'd love it if my dad were a vet."

Hope slung her knapsack over her shoulder. "It's okay, I guess." She didn't seem very excited about it.

"Could I come over sometime and see his office?" I said. "I think my cat, Adelaide, is due for a checkup pretty soon."

A strange look crossed Hope's face. "Oh, well, he's pretty busy. You'd have to make an appointment," she said.

"Oh, of course," I said. I got the feeling that Hope didn't want me to come over to her house. I wasn't trying to invite myself somewhere, but I was just excited about meeting a real veterinarian and seeing the animals. "There's no rush," I assured her as we walked out of Sweet Stuff. "She has all the shots she needs. Hey," I said, trying to get the subject back on the right track, "don't you think the Valentine's party is going to be fun? Everyone's working really hard on it."

"I guess so," Hope said. "I don't know if it's my kind of thing, though."

It was obvious something was bothering her. Somehow, something I had said had ruined the afternoon. And we'd been having so much fun! I could have kicked myself. I had botched the whole thing by pressuring her into inviting me over to her house.

But *why* would that bother her? I wondered. Maybe it was true that she was hiding something, like Kate thought. But what? And why did it make her so sad?

"I can't believe you didn't tell us!" Kate cried that night as we gathered in her room to make valentines.

"Well, I thought Hope wouldn't want to go if it was a big group," I told them.

"Okay, okay, so what did you find out?" Stephanie asked.

"Well, she has a little brother who's five, and her father is a veterinarian," I said. "Her mom works, too. I'm not sure what she does. Anyway, they moved here because her dad grew up in Riverhurst."

"Maybe my dad knows him," Lauren said.

"Maybe. Anyway, we had a good time," I said. "I think Hope's going to fit in fine here, once she gets used to it. She's really nice." Then I told them about how Hope had talked with Horace and made him feel better about being different.

"She does sound nice," Lauren commented when I was finished.

"I bet her advice will work, too," said Stephanie. "It's too bad that she feels like such an outsider."

"It's probably because Jenny Carlin keeps making fun of her," Kate said.

"Maybe we could invite her to one of our sleepovers sometime," I suggested. We don't usually have guests at our sleepovers, but I thought it would make Hope feel more welcome.

"Yeah, then she'd feel like part of a group," Stephanie agreed. "Or at least a good friend."

"Do you think she'd come?" Lauren asked. "She hasn't been exactly jumping at the chance to do stuff with us."

"She might come," I said. "Anyway, there's no harm in asking."

"That's right," Kate said in a determined voice. "You know what else we can do? We can ask her to start eating lunch with us. Then, it'll be perfectly natural for us to ask her what she's doing after school. And then — "

"Kate!" we all cried at once.

She stopped talking and looked confused. "What?"

"We can't *plan* how we're going to become better friends with her," Stephanie said. "That's not the way you make friends."

"Anyway," I said, smiling, "we can't push Hope into being friends with us. She definitely doesn't like being pressured, I can tell."

"Those California people are laid-back about everything," Stephanie said.

"Well, let's just be extra nice to her," Kate said, "and kind of speed things along. If we leave it up to Hope to make friends with us, we'll be waiting forever! It took her two whole weeks to even go out for ice cream with one of us." She frowned. I could tell Kate was hurt that Hope had agreed to go to Sweet Stuff with me instead of her.

"Actually, we had Tofutti," I said.

"Speaking of food, let's get our valentines done before the pizza gets here," Stephanie said. "The last thing I need is tomato sauce all over my secret valentine!"

"What do you mean, your *secret* valentine?" Lauren demanded.

Stephanie picked up the scissors and started cutting a piece of construction paper. "It's a secret."

"A secret named Taylor Sprouse," said Kate.

"No, it's not Taylor." Stephanie picked up the bottle of glue. "What are all of you watching me for, anyway? You have your own cards to make."

I glanced at my watch. "I'd better hurry — I have to be home by seven-thirty." I stared at the paper in front of me. It's always hard to decide whose card to make first. I decided I'd start with Horace's. He wouldn't notice if it was lopsided, and my first few cards were bound to be my worst. I had a long list of people I wanted to give valentines to: my parents, Kate, Stephanie, Lauren, Mrs. Mead, Hope . . . and *maybe* Henry. Maybe. I hadn't decided yet.

We worked in silence for a few minutes — well, not in complete silence because we were listening to the radio, but no one said anything.

"Rats!" Kate suddenly exclaimed.

I looked up and saw her trying to glue two halves of a heart back together.

"I get it," said Lauren. "It's a broken heart!"

Kate glared at her. "It's not supposed to be," she said.

"That's a really good idea," Stephanie said. "You could say something like, 'Don't break my heart, be my Valentine.' "

79

Kate grinned. "Actually, I had that planned all along."

"Yeah, right." Lauren nodded. "Stephanie to the rescue, as usual."

"Look!" Stephanie held up her first card. She had glued lots of tiny red and white hearts onto pink construction paper so that they formed a big heart. Then she had glued white doily paper around the edges of the heart.

"Wow," Lauren breathed. She showed us *her* card. It was a heart folded in half — at least I think it was. "Kind of makes this look like garbage-can material, doesn't it?"

"What *is* that?" Kate asked her.

"How's yours, Patti?" Stephanie asked me.

I shrugged. "It won't win any awards, but Horace won't mind."

"Horace!" Lauren cried. "I thought you were making a card for Henry."

"Not yet," I said.

"Oh, so you're *going* to," Stephanie said meaningfully. "Right?"

"*You* just don't want to be the only person who sends a secret valentine," Kate said, shaking her head. "Some secret, anyway."

"Look, if I was making a valentine for Taylor, it wouldn't be red and pink," Stephanie pointed out.

Taylor's favorite color is black — he dresses in black every day, as if he were going to a funeral.

"Can you imagine giving someone a black valentine?" Lauren laughed. "It's like giving someone a black rose."

"Maybe if you gave Wayne Miller a black rose, he'd take the hint and leave you alone," Kate said, giggling.

"Or else make him a valentine that says 'Get lost,' and sign it, 'Your Secret Un-Admirer,' " Stephanie sputtered.

"Don't even say *Valentine* and his *name* in the same sentence!" Lauren shrieked.

Listening to Lauren's reaction to Wayne liking her made me even more uneasy about giving Henry a valentine. Just thinking about it made my stomach start to hurt. What if he didn't like me the same way I liked him? It would definitely have to be a secret. I didn't even want to use my handwriting on it.

Then I got an idea. If I cut up words from a magazine and used the letters on the card, he wouldn't know *who* it was from. I grabbed a magazine off the table and started skimming through it for the right letters.

"What are you doing?" Kate asked me.

"Never mind," I said, winking at Stephanie. "It's a secret."

Chapter 9

"Happy Valentine's Day!" Mrs. Mead said cheerfully. "Look at all of your costumes! This is terrific!"

"Check out *her* costume," Henry whispered to me. "Talk about sappy!" Mrs. Mead was wearing a red sweater and a red skirt, and she had a big heart-shaped rhinestone pin on her sweater.

I looked at Henry out of the corner of my eye. He was wearing clothes almost identical to the ones he had worn for the float — a leather jacket, jeans with the cuffs rolled up, white socks, and black shoes. He had some kind of gel in his hair, too. I thought he looked pretty cute.

I wished I were as happy about what I was wearing. I had on the poodle skirt, a white blouse, and a cardigan sweater. My mom had curled my hair under at the bottom, and I had pink bobby socks and sneakers on — just like Stephanie had suggested. I thought it was a cute outfit for the dance — but it felt pretty funny wearing it in our classroom. I was glad a lot of other kids were dressed up, too.

Lauren was wearing her regular jeans and one of those sweater sets — you know, one sweater on top of the other. She didn't look very fifties to me. She looked sort of confused, like the top half of her was in the fifties and the rest wasn't. Kate had tracked down an authentic fifties dress for the occasion. It fit tightly at the waist and then the skirt flared out. I thought it looked sort of silly, but then again, I was the one wearing a bright pink skirt with a huge "P" on it. On my way into class I held my books over the letter so no one would notice it.

Stephanie was the only one of us who looked like she was ready for a Valentine's Day party. She had on a red shirt with big black polka dots, a pair of black pants that ended just above her ankles, which she called "pedal pushers," and black flats (with no socks, even though it was February. She said sometimes you had to suffer to be fashionable). Her hair was pulled up into a ponytail with a red ribbon. There was no question in my mind as to who would win the costume contest!

It certainly wouldn't be Hope. She was wearing

the same hippie-style clothes she wore every day. She wasn't the only one who hadn't dressed up, though. A bunch of the boys were wearing their regular old stuff. That only made me worry more about my dumb skirt. I'm never letting Stephanie talk me into wearing something like this again.

Lunch was a real riot because almost everyone in fifth and sixth grade was dressed up, and everyone who *wasn't* dressed up — the fourth-graders, mostly — kept gawking at us like we were aliens from Pluto. I was shuffling through the lunchline when I heard Jenny and Angela cackling behind me. I turned around to see what they were laughing at.

"I thought this was a *fifties* party," Jenny said. "But some people around here are stuck in the sixties!"

Hope was standing behind Jenny, and her face turned bright red.

"I mean, the last time I saw anyone wearing a bandanna was in this old movie about a bunch of hippies. And they had tie-dyed shirts on, too!" Jenny added.

Hope was wearing an oversized tie-dyed shirt with all kinds of bright and wild colors in it, and a bandanna around her waist, like a belt. I liked it.

Stephanie looked at Jenny and shook her head.

"Actually, those shirts are really popular now," she informed her. "But you wouldn't know that, would you?"

"All I know is, this is supposed to be a costume party, and some people think they're too good to dress up for it," Jenny said in a snooty tone, loud enough for Hope to hear. "I think that anyone who isn't dressed for a sock hop shouldn't be allowed to come!"

"It's a free country," Kate said. "*Anyone* can come to the party, dressed up or not! It's none of your business how other people dress."

"Yeah — you should spend more time worrying about your own clothes!" Stephanie added. She turned back around, her ponytail swinging. I thought I saw a little smile on Hope's face. I was glad my friends had stuck up for her, even if I was a little intimidated by Jenny.

Jenny was fuming. She started to say something else, but we just grabbed our trays and headed over to our table.

"What nerve," Lauren said when we sat down.

"I know!" Stephanie agreed. "There she is cutting down someone else's clothes when *she* looks like she got dressed in the dark!"

I took a bite of a heart-shaped cookie. "Even the cafeteria went all out for Valentine's Day," I said.

"Hey, are you guys ready to hand out your valentines?" asked Lauren.

I bit my lip. "I don't know. How are you supposed to give someone a secret valentine and keep it a secret?"

"Slip it into their desk, silly!" Stephanie advised. "The same way you give everyone else their valentines."

"Oh. But what if someone sees you?" I asked.

"Say you're doing it as a favor for a friend," said Lauren. "But don't use my name, whatever you do!"

Just then, I noticed that Hope was standing at the lunchroom door looking confused, as if she didn't know where to sit. She was holding a brown bag and a carton of juice.

"I'm going to ask her to sit with us," I said. I walked over to her. "Hi!" I said. "Happy Valentine's Day!"

"Thanks," she said. "Same to you."

"Why don't you sit with us?" I asked. "I mean, if you don't have other plans."

Hope smiled. "Sure," she said. She followed me back to the table and we sat down. "Hi," Hope said shyly. She pulled a sandwich out of her bag.

"What's that?" Stephanie asked.

"Um, sprouts and tofu-spread on whole grain bread." Hope took a bite. "Umm, I'm starving!"

Lauren put down her fork. She looked like she had lost her appetite. It didn't sound all that appealing to me, either.

"I like your costumes," Hope said softly.

"You *are* coming to the party, right?" Stephanie said. "Jenny's wrong — you don't have to dress up in order to go. Lots of kids aren't. And it'll just make it easier for *me* to win Best Costume."

"Modest, isn't she?" Lauren remarked.

"Well, are you coming or not?" Kate demanded. Leave it to Kate to get straight to the point.

Hope shrugged. "I'm not sure. I guess," she mumbled.

"You *have* to be there," Stephanie said. "There's going to be great music to dance to. I hope so, anyway. The sixth grade better not mess it up."

"I don't really dance," Hope admitted.

"That's okay," I told her. "We can stand by the punch bowl and look at all the costumes."

"Watch everyone embarrass themselves," Lauren added with a grin.

"I don't know," Hope said. "I'll see."

"Do you have to go home right after school?" Stephanie asked.

"No," Hope said coldly. "That's not it."

Stephanie looked taken aback. I was kind of surprised by Hope's reaction, too. Stephanie had obviously hit a nerve, the same way I had the other day.

"Well, I'll see you guys later," Hope said, standing to go. She hadn't even finished her lunch.

"Did I say something wrong?" Stephanie asked once Hope was gone.

"I don't think so," I said. "I guess she's just moody."

"If she comes to the party, she'll cheer up," Kate predicted.

"Maybe," I said. But I had a feeling that whatever was bothering Hope wouldn't be solved by a Valentine's party. Especially not if she was still missing her old school, and her best friend.

We ran around after lunch and put our valentines in people's desks. Since everyone else was doing the same thing, no one noticed when I slipped my secret card into Henry's desk. I *hoped* not, anyway.

The afternoon was kind of a waste. No one paid any attention because we were all counting the minutes until two o'clock when the party would start. Finally, at five minutes to two, Mrs. Mead gave up and told us we could go down to the gym.

"Let's check our valentines before we go," Stephanie said.

"Oh, gross!" Lauren said as she sifted through

her valentines. "Look at this." One of the envelopes had *W. Miller* written in the upper lefthand corner. "Hey — what's this?" she said, picking up another card. "I don't recognize the writing. 'From a Secret Admirer,' " she read out loud.

"Let me see!" Stephanie cried. She stared at the card, trying to figure out who had sent it.

"Yeah, I got one without a name on it, too," Kate said, stacking her valentines in a neat pile. "You haven't checked your desk, Patti," she added.

I stuck my hand into my desk slowly. The thing I was most afraid of was not getting *any* valentines. Lucky for me, there were a few lying on top of my books. I skimmed through them until I found the one I was looking for. "It's from Henry," I whispered. I could feel myself blushing.

"That's great!" Lauren said, grinning.

"Yeah, but I didn't sign the one I gave him," I said worriedly. "What if he thinks I didn't give him one?"

"He won't," Stephanie said with a wave of her hand.

"But how will he know?" I asked. I was always doing the wrong thing. I wished I'd signed my name!

"He'll know," Lauren said. "And if he doesn't, you can tell him."

"No way!" I said.

"Come *on*, you guys, we're going to miss the first song," Kate said, pointing to the clock.

"Wait, I haven't looked for mine yet," Stephanie said. She kneeled on the floor and cautiously peered into her desk.

Kate laughed. "Were you expecting them to shower out all over you or something?"

"A tragedy occurred today at Riverhurst Elementary," said Lauren, pretending to hold a microphone, "when a fifth-grade girl was buried by a pile of valentines. They're still attempting to dig her out."

Stephanie didn't pay any attention to their teasing. She was too busy leafing through her cards. "Yes!" she suddenly squealed. She turned to face us. "*Three* secret admirers, thank you very much."

"Okay, okay, so you hold the record," Lauren said. "Let's get to the party!"

When we stepped through the doorway into the gym, I opened my eyes wide. I couldn't believe what a good decorating job they had done. It wasn't a smelly old gym any more — it was a diner! They had squared off part of the gym with the bleachers to make a smaller space for our party. There were some booths, a phony jukebox, and lots of posters from the fifties.

Lauren squeezed my arm. "Ready to hop till you drop?"

Just then, the first song blasted out of the speakers. Mrs. Mead ran over to the sixth-graders who were manning the stereo. She was waving her arms and pointing to her ears. I didn't recognize the song. It sure didn't sound like anything I had ever danced to before.

"This is going to be some adventure," Kate said, peering around the gym. The sixth-grade boys were standing off to one side, staring at everyone who walked in — which happened to be us, at that moment.

I held my hands over my bright pink skirt. What if Henry thought I looked stupid . . . what if he wished he had never sent me a valentine . . . what if he never realized who his secret admirer was . . . what if . . .

"Come on, Patti," Stephanie cried, and pulled me further into the gym.

Chapter
10

"This song is about doing the mashed potato," Kate said. "Is that a dance?"

"I don't know, but I don't think I want to dance, anyway," Lauren said.

"Me neither!" I said. So far the sock hop was turning out to be more like a sock snooze. The sixth-graders kept arguing about which records to play, so there was about a five-minute break in between songs. And they hadn't even played any of the "classic" songs on our *Hits from the Fifties* tape.

Not that it would matter much, because all the boys were standing on one side of the room, and all the girls were on the other. Naturally the boys were hogging the refreshment table, too, so we didn't even get a chance to eat the great food everyone had brought.

"At least the decorations are good," I told Stephanie during the next music break.

"It doesn't matter — this party is a total bore," she grumbled. "We worked so hard on it and the stupid sixth-graders are ruining the whole thing."

It was true. Oh well, at least I didn't have to worry about Henry asking me to dance. *Nobody* was dancing.

"This is ridiculous!" Stephanie fumed. "I'm going to go make a request." She hurried over to the stereo. First she smiled. Then she frowned. Then she started arguing with the sixth-graders.

She walked back to us with a victorious smile. "Ta-da! Get ready to move those hips."

A few seconds later Elvis Presley's voice came booming out of the speakers. Stephanie grabbed Lauren's arm and pulled her out into the center of the "diner." Kate followed, and they started twisting and turning in time to the music.

"Come on, Patti!" Stephanie yelled. She danced over to me and pulled me out onto the floor.

When I looked around at the end of the song, I couldn't believe my eyes. There were lots of people dancing — well, lots of girls, anyway. The boys were still standing at the refreshment table, munching away. Henry and his friends looked like they were about to start a game of basketball at the other end of the gym.

Lauren followed my gaze. "Who needs them, anyway!" she yelled as the next song started.

"Right!" I answered. I took off my sneakers and started hopping around the floor. Who needed Henry now? I was having fun anyway! Still, I couldn't help watching him out of the corner of my eye.

We danced like crazy for the next half hour or so. Stephanie kept showing us different steps, and once we formed a big chain with the other girls and hopped around the room. I could see a couple of the guys tapping their feet, like they wanted to join in, but none of them would make the first move.

"I wonder if dances are like this in high school," Kate said when we sat down to take a break.

I rubbed my left foot. Dancing in socks was dangerous — someone had hopped right on top of it. "I could use something to drink," I said, wiping my forehead.

We made our way through the crowd of dancers to the refreshment table. "It looks like a bomb just hit!" Stephanie complained. Almost all the food was gone, and what was left was lying in bits and pieces around the table.

"I think I see half a cookie," Lauren said.

"Wait a second!" I said. Across the gym, I saw Ms. Gilberto carrying a large plate in one hand and a tin in the other. "The reserves are coming."

"All right!" Kate cried when Ms. Gilberto set down the plate in front of us. It had cookies of all shapes and sizes, with pink icing.

"Thanks," I said, grabbing a cookie. Then I saw Hope, standing off to one side with some other girls from our class. I took another cookie off the plate and headed over to her.

"Hi," she said when I walked up. "Thanks for the valentine. Sorry I didn't get you one."

"That's okay," I said. "Here, have a cookie before the boys devour them all."

We stood next to each other, chewing our cookies and watching people dance, for what seemed like forever. Every once in a while I'd turn to Hope and smile, but I couldn't think of anything to say. And I didn't want to open my big mouth and say something to upset her, like I'd done at Sweet Stuff.

Lauren and Stephanie were back out on the dance floor, hamming it up, and they danced over to where Hope and I were standing. "Come on," Lauren urged, "it's a jitterbug!"

"Do you want to dance?" I asked Hope. Then

I realized how silly that sounded! "I mean, you know, with all of us?"

"No thanks," she said shyly.

"Are you sure?" I said. "If I can do it, you can!"

Hope shook her head. "I think I'll just stay here."

I didn't get the chance to say anything else because Lauren grabbed my arm and spun me around.

At about three-thirty Mrs. Mead took the microphone. "Before the last dance of the day, we have two very special prizes to award," she said.

Stephanie, who was standing in front of me, turned around and gave me the thumbs-up sign.

"For Best Costume, that is," Mrs. Mead continued. "The students who most accurately reflected the fifties sock hop look will each win a gift certificate to Cinema Central." She beamed at the crowd. "Now, is everybody ready?"

A bunch of kids cheered. The mood of the party had really picked up in the last twenty minutes. I think it was because the sixth-grade girls took over the stereo, and they picked much better songs than the boys! The music was so good that some of the boys had even danced — after Mr. Civello got out there and made a fool of himself. But not Henry. I hadn't even talked to him once — I had just known this was going to happen. I figured I'd never know if he liked my valentine.

"The winner in the boys' category is . . . Taylor Sprouse!" Mrs. Mead announced.

"Yo, Sprouse!" his friends called out as he accepted the prize. He did look pretty good in his leather jacket, and cool sunglasses. Stephanie was grinning from ear to ear.

"Just think, if he wins and *you* win," Lauren whispered to Stephanie. "How romantic!"

Stephanie just nodded. Her eyes were glazed over, just like when she watches a Kevin DeSpain movie.

"And in the girls' division, the best costume was worn by Christy Soames!" Mrs. Mead smiled and held out the envelope to Christy, who was wearing a pretty fifties-style dress.

Stephanie's grin disappeared in a hurry. "Can you believe that?" she grumbled, shaking her head. "That figures. She never thinks about anything except clothes!"

I put my hand over my mouth to keep from laughing.

"Steph, I know someone else like that," Lauren said, smiling.

"Yeah, I know her very well," Kate added.

"Long dark curly hair, only dresses in three colors — "

"Well, at least I don't go around fixing contests," Stephanie huffed. She pointed at Christy. "Tell me her outfit's better than mine!"

"And now for the last dance," Mrs. Mead said. "I want everyone to get out there. Happy Valentine's Day!"

Kate looked at Lauren, who looked at me, and I looked at Stephanie. "Well, I guess it's us again," Stephanie said with a sigh.

"Not exactly a *romantic* Valentine's Day, but it's been fun," said Lauren, shuffling out into the center of the room.

I felt a tap on my shoulder. I whirled around and it was — Henry!

"Hey, darlin'," he said, doing an imitation of Elvis. He turned up the collar of his leather jacket. "Want to dance?"

"Uh, sure," I said just as the music started. I couldn't believe it!

Henry slipped his sunglasses on and I laughed. He looked just like Lauren had looked the night she'd dressed up!

"What's so funny?" Henry yelled above the music.

"Nothing!" I yelled back, still giggling. I still

couldn't believe it. I was dancing with Henry, on Valentine's Day. It was the best party ever!

"You two were so cute together!" Stephanie said, slipping into her long winter coat.

"And just think — you danced with Elll-vis," Lauren drawled.

"It was fun," I admitted. I tied the laces on my sneakers. Actually, I couldn't have wished for a better Valentine's Day. I was going to remember it for a long, long, time. There was only one thing bothering me.

"I think everyone had a good time . . ." I said. "Except maybe Hope."

"Yeah, I noticed her standing off to the side," Kate said. "But she stayed for the whole party, so at least she's trying to be sociable."

Stephanie shrugged. "I guess this just isn't her kind of thing."

"Maybe we could ask her to do something this weekend," I suggested. "She looks so lonely!"

Kate snapped her fingers. "I know! We can do what we did when you moved to town, Patti. Remember?"

Stephanie said, "We took you all over town, went to the mall — "

" — and showed you all the other Riverhurst

hot spots," Lauren added with a grin.

"That's right. Why didn't we think of this before?" I asked. I glanced across the gym. Hope was on her way out the door. "If we hurry, we can catch her," I said.

We rushed over. "Hope!" I called out. "Wait up!"

She stopped in the hallway and turned around.

"We want to invite you to a special, all-expenses-paid, trip-of-a-lifetime, whirlwind tour of Riverhurst," Lauren said with a flourish.

"What she means is, we'd like to show you around town tomorrow, if you're interested," I said.

"We can go to lunch at the mall and if it's nice out, ride our bikes to the park," Stephanie added.

"You do have a bike, don't you?" Kate asked.

"Sure," Hope said with a little smile.

"Sure, you'll come, or sure, you have a bike?" asked Stephanie eagerly.

"Both, I guess." Hope said. She seemed a little unsure about it, but she was willing to take the chance.

"Great!" I said. "Where should we meet?"

"How about just inside the front entrance to the mall?" Stephanie suggested.

"Okay," said Hope. "What time?"

"Ten o'clock," Kate said.

"Better make it ten-thirty," added Lauren.

"Sure," Hope said again. She stared at her feet for a second. "I have to get going. So, I'll, um, see you tomorrow."

"Right," Stephanie said.

"Happy Valentine's Day!" I called out as Hope walked off down the hall.

She turned around and gave me a little wave, as we headed to our lockers.

"Gee! I don't know if all these are going to fit in my knapsack." Stephanie grinned and held up a stack of valentines.

"Oh, puh-lease," Kate groaned.

Chapter
11

I went home and changed after school. It felt good to get out of that skirt, even though it had been a fun day. Then I took my valentines out of my book bag and arranged them on my dresser. I must have looked at Henry's about a thousand times. There wasn't anything special about it. In fact, it was pretty silly and had a dumb joke on it. But I didn't care what it looked like. And we had actually danced together, too.

While I was sitting on my bed looking at it, Horace barged into my room. "Look at all the candy I got!" he bragged.

"Where'd you get all that?" I asked as he dumped a fistful of candy hearts onto my bedspread.

"From school!" he said, as if it should have been obvious.

"From kids in your class?"

Horace nodded. "And from my friends in first grade." He popped a heart into his mouth.

"So does that mean that things at school are going better?" I asked hesitantly. I didn't want to say the wrong thing and spoil his good mood.

"Yup," Horace said proudly. "I did what you said. When they call me a genius, I just agree. When they say I'm a shrimp, I agree." He ate another piece of candy. "No problem!"

I was stunned. Horace was acting happier than he had in the past month! "So you don't want to quit school any more?" I asked him.

"I never said I wanted to quit school," he said. "Why would I want to do that? Jerry's going to teach me how to play baseball when spring comes. He says I would make a great shortstop."

I grinned. "A shortstop, huh? Sounds good."

"I'm going to show Mom how much candy I got," Horace announced. He dashed out of my room, leaving a little pile of candy hearts on my bed. I knew I should wait till after dinner, but I figured I'd just have one. I picked up a green one and read the message. It said, NOT NOW. I laughed out loud.

Around seven o'clock I headed over to Stephanie's house. I love our sleepovers at Stephanie's.

She has her own little house in the backyard — she calls it her apartment — that her parents had built so she could have a place of her own. She doesn't live out there, but whenever we have a sleepover we have it in the playhouse. It's really cool. She has two pull-out couches, a TV and VCR, a phone, and a little refrigerator.

"Wow!" I said when Stephanie opened the door. "I should have known. The place looks great!" The apartment was decorated with red and pink streamers, and Stephanie had made a big sign that said *Be My Valentine*.

Stephanie nodded. "Come on in!"

Kate and Lauren were already sprawled on one of the sofas. "I think I sock-hopped too much," Lauren said, rubbing her shins.

"Well, don't fall asleep," Stephanie advised her. "You don't want to miss out on anything."

I looked at Stephanie, puzzled. "What have you got planned?"

"An all-out Valentine celebration," she said with a mischievous smile.

"Meaning?" Kate asked.

"You'll see," Stephanie said mysteriously. "First, I want to give you all your cards." She pulled three boxes out from underneath the sofa and handed one to each of us.

"Kind of big for a card," Lauren said, shaking the box.

I untied the pink ribbon and tore off the wrapping paper. Inside the box was a pair of white socks with red and black hearts on them. "These are great," I told Stephanie. "Thanks!"

"Where did you get them?" Kate asked, holding hers up. "I love them!"

"I made them with paint sticks," Stephanie explained.

"I'm going to put mine on right now," Lauren said, taking off her shoes.

Stephanie pulled up her jeans leg and showed us she was wearing the same socks. "It's what *everyone* in Riverhurst will be wearing this season," she laughed.

"I brought something that will look really good with those," said Kate, reaching into her bag. "I didn't get a chance to wrap them yet, but . . ." She handed each of us a pair of shoelaces with little red hearts on them.

"Those are wild!" Stephanie exclaimed. She yanked her old shoelace out of her sneaker and started threading the new one through the holes.

"Thanks, Kate," I said. "They're great! And . . ." I rummaged around in my knapsack. "They go perfectly with these." I handed everyone a small heart pin. I had picked them up at the drugstore the night before.

Lauren attached the pin to the collar of her jean jacket. "I'm going to be so coordinated, no one will recognize me."

"Thanks, Patti!" Stephanie put the pin on her sweater. "It's one of my *favorite* colors."

"Okay, Lauren, what did you bring?" Kate asked.

"Well . . . it's not exactly something you can wear," Lauren said. "Of course, you could, if you wanted to." She picked up a box and put it on the table. "Ta-da!" she cried, lifting the lid.

Inside were eight chocolate cupcakes covered with pink frosting and decorated with tiny, heart-shaped cinnamon candies. Stephanie lifted one out and took a big bite. "Delish!" she said through a mouthful of crumbs.

"Did you get these at Marino's?" asked Kate.

Lauren folded her arms across her chest. "No, I made them," she said, pretending to be offended. "From a mix, but I made them."

"They're excellent," I said, nodding.

"And the best thing is there are two for each of us," said Kate, grabbing a second cupcake.

Lauren put a hand on Kate's arm. "No, I didn't say that. You each get one — and I get *four*."

"No you don't," Kate said, laughing and snatching the box.

"Okay, are you guys ready for the next surprise?" asked Stephanie.

"That depends," I said. "What is it?"

"A special Valentine's edition of Truth or Dare," Stephanie said with a grin. "And I pick you first, Patti."

"Gee, I'm kind of thirsty," I said, swallowing. "Does anyone else want a soda?"

"No stalling allowed," Stephanie said. "Truth or dare?"

"You're not going to make me do something embarrassing, are you?" I asked. That was a stupid question. Stephanie always thinks up humiliating dares.

"You'll just have to take your chances," Stephanie said, a wicked gleam in her eye.

"Truth then," I said, chickening out.

"If you could have your choice between dancing with Kevin DeSpain, or dancing with Henry, who would you choose?"

"That's easy," I said. "Ke — " Well, maybe it wasn't so easy. I didn't really know Kevin DeSpain at all. I mean, I had met him once, when he was in Riverhurst filming a movie, but still. Henry I actually knew. He was real. And even though Henry went a little overboard trying to imitate Elvis, he was a pretty good dancer. But I couldn't admit I liked him *more* than our favorite movie star! Could I?

Sometimes I hate Truth or Dare!

I took a deep breath. "Henry," I mumbled.

"I knew it!" Stephanie exclaimed.

Lauren was walking back from the fridge. "It's true love," she said dramatically, swooning onto the couch.

"Okay, Stephanie, truth or dare," I said. I wanted to change the subject, fast!

"Dare," she said, trying to sound nonchalant.

"I want you to call Taylor and ask if he was one of your secret admirers," I said.

Stephanie's face turned pale. "You can't make me do that."

"Why not?" asked Kate. "You're the one who planned the *special* Valentine's Truth or Dare."

"Kate's right," said Lauren. She pointed to the phone. "Go ahead. It's 1-800-TAYLOR, I think."

We all burst out laughing.

"Ready for lunch?" Kate asked when we walked out of Just Juniors. We had spent the morning showing Hope our favorite stores in the mall. She seemed to be having a pretty good time.

"What do you feel like eating?" I asked her. "It's our treat."

"Yeah," Kate said. "This tour is 'all expenses paid'!"

"We usually grab a pizza," Lauren told Hope. "But if you don't like pizza, we could go somewhere else. They have salads at — "

"Pizza's great," Hope interrupted. "I just don't eat meat."

I looked at Lauren and shrugged. We always get double-cheese with pepperoni, meatballs and onions. "How about a double-cheese — with onions and green peppers?" I suggested.

"Sounds good to me," said Kate. "Let's go!"

"Have you ever had pineapple on pizza?" Hope asked me as we walked to Pizza Palace.

"No," I said. "It sounds funny — is it good?"

"I like it," Hope said. "But then, I like broccoli and spinach on pizza, too." She laughed.

Lauren stuck out her tongue. "Let's just go with the double-cheese, okay?" She smiled at Hope.

"You have to understand, Lauren's idea of a perfect meal is chocolate, chocolate, and maybe a little peanut butter thrown in," said Stephanie.

"Well, here we are . . . Riverhurst's most famous restaurant!" Lauren announced. As usual, Pizza Palace was jammed with kids playing video games, talking, and laughing.

"This reminds me of a place back home," said Hope, smiling.

"Only in California, all the guys would be wearing surfing shorts," Stephanie said.

"And we'd be tan!" I said.

After lunch we went to Clothing Classics, the antique clothes store. Hope loved it. She bought an old blazer and a cool hat that looked great over her long blonde hair. Then we rode our bikes around town for an hour or so, showing her the skating rink and the park.

At three o'clock, Hope said she had to go home and look after her little brother.

"My parents are going out tonight, too," said Stephanie, "and I have to watch the twins."

"Speaking of little brothers," I said, "Horace is doing great, thanks to you, Hope."

"Me? What did I do?" she asked.

"You told him it was okay to be different, and you also gave me that idea about just agreeing with kids who tease him. Now he has a couple of friends, and the others aren't teasing him so much! He's really happy. He even got a bunch of valentines," I told her.

Stephanie grinned. "I knew he'd get out of that mess okay."

"What are you guys doing tomorrow?" asked Lauren.

"Maybe we could catch a matinee at Cinema Central," Kate recommended.

"If *I* had won that stupid gift certificate like I *should* have, I could pay for all of us," Stephanie complained.

"I have an idea," said Hope shyly. "Why don't you come over to my house for lunch? I owe you one."

I saw Kate's eyes light up. I was intrigued, too.

"We'd love to come over," Kate answered for all of us.

"Okay. It's 146 Birch Street," Hope said, climbing onto her mountain bike. "Come over around twelve. Thanks for the tour!" She started riding off down the street.

"I can't wait for tomorrow!" Kate said once she was gone. "The mystery will finally be solved."

Lauren looked confused. "I didn't know there still was one."

"Sure — aren't you dying to see what her house is like?" asked Kate.

I shrugged. "I guess. But I feel like we already

know everything we need to know about Hope."

"Me, too," said Stephanie. "I like her."

"I do, too," said Kate. "But you know, you can tell a lot *more* about a person by seeing their house."

Lauren rolled her eyes. "Kate's going to forget about being a movie director and become a detective instead," she predicted. "Kate Beekman, P.I."

"It's better than Lauren Hunter, Bottomless P.I.T.," Kate said with a giggle.

Chapter 12

"This is it!" Kate said, jumping off her bike.

Hope's house turned out to be less than five minutes from Lauren's. It looked fairly average, except that it had a long extension on one side. "That must be her father's office," I said.

We put our bikes in the driveway and rang the front doorbell. There were wind chimes on the front porch, and they made a beautiful, tinkling sound.

"Hi!" said Hope, opening the door. "Come on in!"

We walked into the living room. There was a huge painting on one wall with big bright orange and yellow splashes that reminded me of something *I* would paint. Their furniture was very simple, and the couch had an Indian-print bedspread thrown over it.

"I'll show you my room," said Hope, and we followed her upstairs.

Her room looked a little bit like Lauren's! There were some clothes on the floor, and piles of books and papers on her desk.

Stephanie pointed to the wall, which was half purple and half white. "I like that."

"Oh." Hope blushed. "Actually, I'm still painting it. It's going to be all purple — well, that wall anyway. I just haven't finished it yet."

"Your parents are letting you paint your own room?" Lauren asked.

"My mother would have a fit if I did that," added Kate.

Hope smiled. "It's probably just a way for my dad to get out of doing it himself. So, are you guys hungry?"

"That depends," said Lauren, laughing. "What's for lunch?"

"I got something you guys will like," Hope said as we traipsed back downstairs. "You said yesterday you like Mexican food, so we can make tacos."

Lauren rubbed her stomach. "In that case, I'm starving!"

We went into the kitchen and Hope got some plates out of the cupboard. "I just have to heat up the taco shells. The stuff is right here." She pointed to bowls of refried beans, tomatoes, cheese, lettuce, salsa — and sprouts.

I heard the front door open and shut, and a few seconds later Hope's father walked into the kitchen. "Hello there," he said, smiling at us. He was wearing jeans and a striped cotton sweater. I was expecting him to have long hair, but he didn't. He looked like any other dad.

"These are my new, um, friends," Hope said. "Patti, Lauren, Kate, and Stephanie."

"Hi," we all said in unison.

"It's very nice to meet you," Dr. Lenski said.

"How was the cow?" Hope asked, sliding a tray into the oven.

"Well, she's not sick — she's just expecting a calf," Dr. Lenski said. "I was out at the Williams' farm this morning," he told us.

"Wow, how exciting," said Lauren.

"Not really," he said. "Not yet, anyway!"

Just then, a little boy with curly blond hair bounded into the room yelling, "Hope, I got to ride on a horse!" He stopped short when he saw all of us.

"That's great, Rain." Hope ruffled his hair. "These are my friends. We're going to have lunch. Do you want some?"

"They gave us lunch at the farm, actually," Dr.

Lenski said, patting his stomach. "I couldn't eat another bite. I think I'll go read the paper. Rain, why don't you work on cleaning up your room? When you finish, we can play a game of something, okay? I'll see you girls later."

Dr. Lenski went into the living room and Rain bolted upstairs.

"Rain's really cute," Stephanie said.

"Yeah, he is," Hope agreed.

"Where's your mom?" I asked. "Is she a veterinarian, too?"

"No," said Hope. "She's just, well, she has to work on Sundays, too."

"I didn't think anyone had to work on Sundays," Lauren said.

"Well, she's working on a special project," Hope said. "So, the tacos should be done soon," she said. She seemed really eager to get off the subject of her mother.

Dr. Lenski suddenly appeared in the doorway. "Hope, can I talk to you?" He didn't look happy.

"Okay, but the tacos are — "

"It'll only take a second."

Hope sighed and put down the oven mitts. "I'll be right back. Don't let the tacos burn."

After she had gone, Lauren whispered, "What's going on?"

"Did we get her in trouble?" Stephanie asked softly.

"I don't know," Kate said with a frown. "You're right, Lauren, hardly anybody works on Sundays. So where *is* her mom?"

Then Hope came back to the kitchen, so I quickly started talking about what had happened that day at breakfast.

"You know how Horace is doing so well in school now, right?" I asked everybody. "You're not going to believe this, but my parents are thinking about moving *me* up a grade."

"What?" Kate demanded.

I nodded. "They told me this morning at breakfast that they think I should. Isn't that crazy?"

"You can't leave 5B," Lauren said. "You're smart enough to, but come on! They can't split us up."

"You'll have to talk them out of it," Stephanie said. "I mean think about it — if you move out of our class, you won't sit next to Henry any more," she reminded me.

That settled it! "I'll definitely talk them out of it," I said. I hoped it was one of those passing things — maybe they'd forget about it by the end of the week. I couldn't count on that, though. My parents aren't very forgetful.

"Everything's ready!" Hope announced. "Come and get it."

"This is really good," Lauren said a few minutes later. "They taste good without the meat."

Stephanie dragged a chip through the salsa. "What kind of salsa is this? I love it — it's so spicy!"

"It's homemade," Hope said.

"You're kidding!" I said.

"Nope, I made it myself. Actually, I got the recipe from a restaurant in San Francisco we always used to go to," Hope explained. "I really miss that place."

The rest of us kept eating, except for Hope, who just sipped her glass of milk and tapped the floor with her moccasins. She seemed to be thinking something over.

"I have to tell you guys something," she finally said.

We all looked up expectantly. This sounded serious.

"I kind of lied when I said my mom was at work," Hope said, looking down at the table. "The truth is, she's in San Francisco."

I bit my lip. So there *was* a secret, after all.

"My parents got a divorce a month ago," she went on. "I guess I just didn't want to talk about it."

"You don't have to feel bad about it," I told her.

"I mean, it's nothing to be embarrassed about."

"It must be tough, though," Lauren said sympathetically.

"Kind of," Hope admitted. "I miss my mom."

"How come you and your dad left San Francisco?" Kate asked. "I mean, if you'd stayed there you could see your mom more."

"I know, but she works a lot — she's a lawyer and she has a really successful practice. My dad has a much more flexible schedule, so he can be here when Rain and I need him. And he's been wanting to move back to Riverhurst for a long time," Hope said.

"I'm glad he did," I told her. I didn't know what else to say. Just recently the parents of Ginger Kinkaid, a girl in 5C, had gotten a divorce. She and her mom had moved to a new house (which happened to be Lauren's old house). But her dad was still nearby. I couldn't imagine having to choose to live with my mom or my dad — and move so far away from the other! No wonder Hope had been so sad. I would be miserable, too.

"I like it here okay," said Hope. "I just wish she were closer. I haven't seen her since we moved, and I probably won't get to until the summer."

"Do you talk to her a lot?" Stephanie asked.

"Practically every night," Hope said with a

119

smile. "She wants to know every detail. I already told her about you all."

"Maybe she'll move closer some day," Lauren said.

Hope shook her head. "I doubt it. She's pretty happy in California."

"Well, I'm sure she misses you as much as you miss her," I told Hope.

"Yeah." Hope stood up and started clearing the table. I got up to help her.

"Does your father cook, or do you?" Stephanie asked.

"My dad does — but that's nothing new. He always did the cooking," Hope said. "He's really good at it. Mom's favorite thing to do is order take-out Chinese food!"

Lauren laughed. "That's how I feel about cooking, too!"

"Look — I got these for dessert," Hope said, taking a box of fruit bars out of the freezer. "They're healthy *and* they're sweet." She handed one to Lauren and grinned. "Sorry, no chocolate coating."

"That's okay," Lauren said. "It probably won't kill me."

Hope tore the wrapper off her fruit bar. "I rented a couple of movies if you guys want to watch one."

"That would be great," Kate said, sitting down

on the Indian-print couch. I grabbed a funky-looking chair, and Lauren and Stephanie sprawled out on the floor. Hope popped the tape into the VCR and sat down next to Kate as the opening credits rolled across the screen.

It felt funny to be a fivesome instead of a foursome — but it felt nice, too.

#33 *Lauren's Double Disaster*

Then Patti turned to me. "How about you, Lauren? What do you think you'll do for the art fair?"

"I'm still not sure," I confessed. Why couldn't jogging or shooting baskets be on the list of projects?

Kate said, "Lauren, we'll help you."

Stephanie frowned. "Why would Lauren need our help? She's got more imagination than any of us."

I couldn't help thinking they were wrong. I was the biggest art klutz in the whole school, and soon everyone was going to know it.

SLEEPOVER FRIENDS™

by Susan Saunders

Available wherever you buy books...or use this order form.

THE BABY-SITTERS CLUB®

by Ann M. Martin

The seven girls at Stoneybrook Middle School get into all kinds of adventures...with school, boys, and, of course, baby-sitting!

❑ NI43388-1	#1	Kristy's Great Idea	$2.95
❑ NI43513-2	#2	Claudia and the Phantom Phone Calls	$2.95
❑ NI43511-6	#3	The Truth About Stacey	$2.95
❑ NI42498-X	#30	Mary Anne and the Great Romance	$2.95
❑ NI42497-1	#31	Dawn's Wicked Stepsister	$2.95
❑ NI42496-3	#32	Kristy and the Secret of Susan	$2.95
❑ NI42495-5	#33	Claudia and the Great Search	$2.95
❑ NI42494-7	#34	Mary Anne and Too Many Boys	$2.95
❑ NI42508-0	#35	Stacey and the Mystery of Stoneybrook	$2.95
❑ NI43565-5	#36	Jessi's Baby-sitter	$2.95
❑ NI43566-3	#37	Dawn and the Older Boy	$2.95
❑ NI43567-1	#38	Kristy's Mystery Admirer	$2.95
❑ NI43568-X	#39	Poor Mallory!	$2.95
❑ NI44082-9	#40	Claudia and the Middle School Mystery	$2.95
❑ NI43570-1	#41	Mary Anne Versus Logan (Feb. '91)	$2.95
❑ NI44083-7	#42	Jessi and the Dance School Phantom (Mar. '91)	$2.95
❑ NI43571-X	#43	Stacey's Revenge (Apr. '91)	$2.95
❑ NI44240-6		Baby-sitters on Board! Super Special #1	$3.50
❑ NI44239-2		Baby-sitters' Summer Vacation Super Special #2	$3.50
❑ NI43973-1		Baby-sitters' Winter Vacation Super Special #3	$3.50
❑ NI42493-9		Baby-sitters' Island Adventure Super Special #4	$3.50
❑ NI43575-2		California Girls! Super Special #5	$3.50

For a complete listing of all the Baby-sitter Club titles write to:
Customer Service at the address below.

Available wherever you buy books...or use this order form.

Scholastic Inc., P.O. Box 7502, 2931 E. McCarty Street, Jefferson City, MO 65102

Please send me the books I have checked above. I am enclosing $ _____
(please add $2.00 to cover shipping and handling). Send check or money order — no cash or C.O.D.s please.

Name _____

Address _____

City _____ State/Zip_____

Please allow four to six weeks for delivery. Offer good in U.S.A. only. Sorry, mail orders are not available to residents of Canada. Prices subject to change.   BSC790